No Reservations About Killing . . .

Longarm did not think he had ever seen the man before. Certainly he was not a patron of the Star Saloon.

But the fellow recognized Longarm. And seemed to fear him.

His hand leaped toward his revolver.

Longarm had no idea why.

But he did not have time to ponder the question or to ask why. The man was drawing on him. That was introduction enough.

Longarm's .45 came to hand almost without him taking time to consciously reach for it.

His Colt spat its own brand of thunder and lightning as flame and smoke—and lead—belched from the muzzle.

Across the width of the café floor Longarm's first bullet took the man in the belly.

A second struck him high in the chest. And a third ripped into the left side of his face.

"Jesus!" Tisbury screamed.

Longarm came to his feet and stood poised to fire again if necessary. A fourth bullet was not needed. The man, a complete stranger [illegible] led. He toppled face-forv[illegible] a sack of grain, making [illegible] are for it. Once he hit, h[illegible]

DON'T MISS THESE ALL-ACTION WESTERN SERIES FROM THE BERKLEY PUBLISHING GROUP

THE GUNSMITH by J. R. Roberts

Clint Adams was a legend among lawmen, outlaws, and ladies. They called him . . . the Gunsmith.

LONGARM by Tabor Evans

The popular long-running series about Deputy U.S. Marshal Custis Long—his life, his loves, his fight for justice.

SLOCUM by Jake Logan

Today's longest-running action Western. John Slocum rides a deadly trail of hot blood and cold steel.

BUSHWHACKERS by B. J. Lanagan

An action-packed series by the creators of Longarm! The rousing adventures of the most brutal gang of cutthroats ever assembled—Quantrill's Raiders.

DIAMONDBACK by Guy Brewer

Dex Yancey is Diamondback, a Southern gentleman turned con man when his brother cheats him out of the family fortune. Ladies love him. Gamblers hate him. But nobody pulls one over on Dex . . .

WILDGUN by Jack Hanson

The blazing adventures of mountain man Will Barlow—from the creators of Longarm!

TEXAS TRACKER by Tom Calhoun

J.T. Law: the most relentless—and dangerous—manhunter in all Texas. Where sheriffs and posses fail, he's the best man to bring in the most vicious outlaws—for a price.

TABOR EVANS

LONGARM AND THE STAR SALOON

JOVE BOOKS, NEW YORK

THE BERKLEY PUBLISHING GROUP
Published by the Penguin Group
Penguin Group (USA) LLC
375 Hudson Street, New York, New York 10014

USA • Canada • UK • Ireland • Australia • New Zealand • India • South Africa • China

penguin.com

A Penguin Random House Company

LONGARM AND THE STAR SALOON

A Jove Book / published by arrangement with the author

For information, address: The Berkley Publishing Group,
a division of Penguin Group (USA) LLC,
375 Hudson Street, New York, New York 10014.

ISBN: 978-0-515-15430-6

PUBLISHING HISTORY
Jove mass-market edition / January 2014

PRINTED IN THE UNITED STATES OF AMERICA

10 9 8 7 6 5 4 3 2 1

Cover illustration by Milo Sinovcic.

Chapter 1

"Pardon me for sayin' this, ma'am, but you got big tits."

"That, sir, is *un*-pardonable. Have you never been taught how to speak to a lady?"

"Yeah, an' if there was a lady present, I wouldn't talk like that."

"You son of a bitch!"

"You old bag."

"Not so old that I couldn't fuck you into the ground, mister."

Longarm threw his head back and laughed. "Yes, an' I believe you could still do it, too."

"Oh, Custis, it *is* good to see you, dear. Thank you for coming."

"Anytime you need me. I told you that once an' I meant it."

Helen Morrow threw her arms around Longarm's neck and clung to him for a few moments before she lifted her face to his and kissed him long and deep.

Helen was a big woman, tall and thick and round. He suspected she would weigh in the neighborhood of three hundred pounds . . . if you could find a scale to take her. A livestock scale perhaps.

But she was all woman. A former lover, although she had been considerably thinner then. And he was genuinely fond of her.

Helen had to rise up only a little to reach Longarm's lips. Then she hugged him and stepped back a pace.

"Let me look at you, dear," she said. "Good Lord, you've hardly changed over the years."

Deputy United States Marshal Custis Long grinned and said, "It's the result o' clean living."

His remark brought a bark of sharp laughter from Helen. She knew better than to believe that. "But you do look fine, dear," she said.

Deputy Long, known as Longarm to friend and foe alike, did indeed look fit. He was tall, well over six feet in height, with broad shoulders and narrow hips.

He had brown hair, a broad sweep of brown mustache, golden brown eyes, and a firm jaw. He wore a brown tweed coat, brown corduroy trousers, and a flat-crowned brown Stetson hat. His gunbelt, rigged for a cross-draw, was polished black, as were his stovepipe cavalry boots. Beneath the coat he wore a calfskin vest with a gold watch chain stretched across his belly.

"I swear, dear, you haven't changed a bit. How long has it been?" Helen asked.

The corners of Longarm's eyes crinkled as he smiled and said, "Too long, darlin'. How've you been? An' why am I here?" The smile widened and he added, "Apart from the pleasure o' seein' you, that is."

"Come into my office, dear. I don't like to talk too openly out here in the parlor where anyone might hear."

Longarm glanced around at the bevy of ladies who were

sitting in the overstuffed chaises, waiting for customers to arrive. He removed his hat and followed Helen down a short hallway and into a large, sumptuously appointed office and bedchamber.

"Would you like something to drink, dear? Rye whiskey, perhaps? I have a good brand. Bought it just for you."

"And I'll enjoy it, I'm sure, but right now what I'd like, if you have some, is a cup o' coffee."

"Right away, dear. Sit down. Make yourself comfortable. I won't be a moment."

Helen left the room, her movements light despite her bulk, and Longarm perched on the side of Helen's big canopy bed. True to her word, Helen was back in less than a minute.

"I thought you were going for coffee," he said.

"You never have had any patience, have you?" The big woman chided him. "It will be here in a minute."

"Oh, my. Servants. You really have come up in the world, haven't you?" he said.

Helen nodded. "I've come a long way since you knew me, dear." She sighed. "A very long way. That has a bearing on why I asked for your help."

"I'm listenin'," he said.

There was a knock at the door, and a slender, doe-eyed girl whose skin tones suggested she might have been Mexican or perhaps Indian entered with a tray containing a carafe of steaming coffee along with cups and condiments. There was also a small plate of butter cookies.

The girl served the coffee, curtsied daintily, and silently left.

Longarm balanced his cup and saucer on his knee and said, "You were sayin'?"

Helen sighed again, and her shoulders slumped wearily. "Custis dear, there are five whorehouses in Quapah County, and I own three of them."

Longarm's eyebrows went up. "Congratulations. No wonder you look so prosperous."

"Oh, I have money, it's true. This is the most elegant of my properties."

He nodded. The house was indeed splendid. And the girls he had seen out in the parlor were handsome, each of them impeccably dressed and made up.

"One of the others is, frankly, a dump. It's a cheap house for cheap whores." She smiled. "And would you believe, I make more money off of it than I do from the other two combined. We have cowboys coming here to ship cattle, railroaders working on the line, and recently we got an influx of coal miners working the newly opened diggings north of town. The men like things simple and cheap, and they don't even seem to mind what the girls look like as long as they are willing to drop their knickers for half a dollar."

"You aren't surprising me none," Longarm said, trying the coffee and finding it very much to his liking. "So what does this have to do with . . . ?"

"Someone is trying to muscle me out, Custis. And I don't even know who is doing it," Helen said.

"They're tryin' to hurt you?" he asked.

She nodded. "Financially, anyway. And there have been . . . suggestions . . . that I could be hurt physically if I don't play along with them."

Longarm smiled. "In that case, darlin', you did the exact best thing when you sent for me, 'cause operators like that are just my meat. Hand me one o' them cookies, will you, please?"

Chapter 2

When he had known her before—long before he became a deputy United States marshal—Helen Morrow had befriended a young out-of-work and out-of-money Custis Long. She took a liking to him and gave him a hand up.

At the time she worked as an accountant for an elderly gentleman. Longarm had suspected she did more for the old fellow than keep his books, but he had never asked and Helen never volunteered any information of that nature.

She had taken him in. Fed him. Washed his clothes. Given him a place to sleep. And fucked him. She had helped him find his way in this brawling, sprawling, wide open Western land, and he had never forgotten her. The way Longarm saw it, he owed her. Anything he could do that would help Helen Morrow, he would do and gladly.

He reached for the carafe and refilled his coffee cup, then said, "If you don't mind me askin', how'd you come by three whorehouses? Back when we were close, you didn't have much more'n I did." He grinned. "And I didn't have hardly nothin' but a ragged shirt and a wore-out pistol."

"I remember that shirt." She laughed. "I had to patch it for you, as I recall."

"You did a fine job of it too. I can recommend you as a seamstress if you get tired o' riding herd on these ladies of the evening."

"Yes. Them," Helen said. "Do you remember Albert, the gentleman I worked for at the time?"

"I remember meeting him. Didn't exactly get to know him, of course, but we met."

"Yes, well, Albert and I were . . . close, you might say. He was married, of course, and had children. Naturally they were the recipients of his estate when he died, but there was a secret . . . I think the word is codicil or something like that. Anyway it was a bequest that he did not want his wife and children to know about.

"He didn't want them to know about quite all of his business ventures, and he certainly did not want them to know about me. So when he died, I inherited a whorehouse. I already knew about it, of course. I had been keeping the books on it for almost a dozen years by that time.

"I had my own ideas about the business side of how to run a house. And I learned the practical side of it. How to hire the girls. And how to fire them when necessary. How to handle the drunks and the brawlers and the ones who couldn't get it up." She smiled. "It might surprise you, Custis, how many there are of those. They come in acting tough and saying they will strap on their spurs and ride a girl into the ground, then when they get to the room, they can't get a proper hard-on. Naturally our rule is that no one ever finds out about those boys. But we know. The truth is that the girls like to have them as customers. Usually they are no trouble at all; they don't want their secret to get out, you see."

Longarm finished his coffee and took the last cookie from the plate.

"It turns out that I have a good head for business," Helen said. "I inherited the one house, but I've worked my way up to own the others as well. And my girls are treated right. I haven't had a suicide in more than a year. Show me one other house that can make that claim. My girls make good money, and they can leave whenever they like. I even give them an address in town where their folks can write to them and think they are working for a hatmaker. Not many of their families know what they really do for a living, of course.

"I've worked hard for my success, Custis," she said. "I would hate to have to start over at my age. I could do it, of course. But I would hate it."

"Then let's make sure it don't come to that," Longarm said. He set his cup aside and went to her. He put his arms around her and held her close. After a moment Helen began to weep silently.

"There, there, darlin'," he said. He fashioned a smile and added, "You did exactly the right thing when you asked me to come lend a hand."

Chapter 3

"Could I have a taste o' that rye whiskey you were talkin' about?" he asked.

"Of course. I have it right here."

Longarm enjoyed rye whiskey. But more than the drink, he wanted to give Helen a task that would help settle her down. It was his experience that nothing benefited a woman more than waiting on a man. It took her mind off whatever had been bothering her so she could concentrate on being helpful.

Helen rose ponderously from her armchair and went to a waist-high cherrywood cabinet at the side of the room. She opened it, took out a bottle and glasses, and poured a generous measure of whiskey for Longarm. Finally she delivered the drink to him and resumed her seat.

"Ah. You were right, darlin'. This is good stuff," he said after trying the whiskey. "The best. Thank you."

"I'm glad you like it," she said.

"Do you feel like talking about your situation now?" he asked after a minute or so.

"Certainly." Helen said.

Longarm took another swallow of the rye and asked, "How exactly is someone trying to undermine you and you don't even know who's doing it?"

"Oh, Custis. It has been horrible. You remember that I told you I have a post office box where the girls' families can write to them?"

He nodded and drained the last of the rye. Helen did not seem to notice. In any event she did not offer to refill the whiskey, so he got up and helped himself to another glass. The rye really was of excellent quality, and he just plain enjoyed the stuff, even though Helen was suffering.

"Someone knows what that box number is, Custis. They are sending threatening letters, some of them really nasty."

"To you?" he asked.

"Yes. And lately to my girls as well."

"Have you saved any of those so I can see what they say?" he asked.

Helen shook her head. "They are . . . They were terrible things. I didn't want them under my roof. They threatened to . . . to do things to us. Ugly, hateful things, Custis. They threatened to mutilate us. Threatened to cut off certain, um, body parts. That sort of thing. I burned the letters. Every one that I had. When they started coming, I didn't know. Wasn't prepared. I just gave the unopened envelopes to the girls." She made a sour face. "That was a mistake."

Longarm grunted. He set his whiskey aside and took out a cheroot, nipped off the twist and spat it out, then struck a match and held the flame to the blunt end of the slender cigar.

"I might have thought it was all a terrible prank," Helen said, "but whoever is writing these letters knows the girls' real names. They use nicknames for their work, of course. All working girls do. But the person who is writing those letters knows the real names of my girls. Some of them are becoming afraid that this person will tell their families where they work." Helen sighed. "It is one thing to be a whore, you see, but quite another thing for one's mother to know. They would hate that, even the girls who have been thrown out of their homes, which is how I get a good many of my girls."

"Have you done anything about the letters?" Longarm asked.

Helen managed a smile. "Aside from asking for your help, you mean? Well, yes. I have. I've started opening all the mail and throwing those letters away before the girls see them. That has helped, of course. But I've already lost some of my best girls because of it. Three from this house. Two from my middle-class house over on Buxton Avenue and four from my hog ranch down by the creek. It is easy enough to replace girls, but this whole thing has them rattled."

"I would imagine so," Longarm said. "I wish you'd saved some of them, but if they're gone, they're gone. Any more that come in, though, I want to see them."

"Of course," Helen said, nodding. She stood and began pacing back and forth across the room. After a few turns around the room she stopped, looked at him, and asked, "Is there anything you can do to help me, Custis?"

He smiled. "It just could be. And in the line o' duty too. I'd think that this jasper using the United States Post Office to make his threats is cause enough for me to take a hand in the game as a deputy as well as as your friend. Now, tell me where I can get something to eat in this town. Then I'll get started and see what, if anything, I can do to help you, darlin'."

Chapter 4

"You can eat here, of course, Custis," Helen said. "Sleep here too if you wish."

"Thanks, but it might be a good idea if I don't let folks in town know that we're such good friends," he told her. "If I come and go, no one will think a thing about it. After all, men do visit whorehouses. But if I were to move in and stay, well, that'd be a whole different kettle o' fish."

"Oh, I see," Helen said. "I hadn't thought of that." She came over to him, leaned down, and kissed him on the cheek. "You've grown, Custis. Not just gotten bigger, I mean. You've grown up. Matured. You were a lovely boy when I knew you. Now you are a man through and through."

"I hope you don't mind the changes," he said, giving her a fond smile.

"I like everything about you." Helen laughed. "Especially that magnificent dick. Oh, I remember that, all right. Biggest damn thing I ever had shoved up my twat."

"Helen, you talk pretty slutty, but I bet you haven't had half a dozen peckers stuck in you your whole life long. Now, fess up. Am I telling the truth there or not? Half a dozen tops," he said.

"Why, Custis. A gentleman does not ask a lady such a thing."

"Shit, Helen, I do. So tell me true. Half a dozen? Less?"

"I am not going to tell you any such thing, Custis Long," she insisted. But he could see from her expression that she was more amused by his question than offended by it.

He stood and gave her a kiss. Considerably more of one than the little buss she had planted on his cheek. "Helen, you know you're lady enough for me. Always have been. Now, tell me. Is there a halfway decent hotel in this town, and where can I find a good meal that doesn't come out o' your kitchen?"

"That is one benefit from being the madam of a whore-house, Custis. I get to know almost everything about my town and the people who live here. So let me tell you what I would recommend . . ."

Half an hour later Longarm had checked into the railside Pickering Hotel and was seated on a stool at the counter of the Tisbury Café, which was across the street half a block from the hotel.

He ordered coffee—it was not half as good as what had come out of Helen's kitchen—and a huge steak with all the trimmings.

Chapter 5

The most essential needs of the inner man satisfied, Longarm ambled along the street until he found a likely looking saloon. That was not a difficult feat in a railroad town. Half the buildings were either saloons or rooming houses.

He pushed through the batwings and inhaled the familiar scents of sawdust, beer, and tobacco smoke.

The place had five round poker tables, only one of them occupied, and an empty faro table at the back. Half a dozen men leaned on the bar. There were no working girls visible although this was what Longarm would have thought was prime time for whores to ply their trade.

"What will you have?" the barman said by way of greeting. The man was balding, probably middle-aged, wearing a sleeveless shirt beneath his apron.

Longarm wondered if the bare arms were because he did not want to get sleeves wet while washing up . . . or to show off muscles that were only beginning to sag and must once have been powerful indeed.

"Beer," Longarm responded. After Helen's superb rye whiskey, he did not want to settle for something less. And any whiskey found behind a public bar like this was bound to be considerably less. "And is that a box of cheroots I see over there by them bottles?"

The bartender nodded. "Aye, and they're good and fresh."

Which they would not remain, Longarm knew, if the man kept them out in an open box like that. They would quickly dry out in this climate. Better to keep them in a humidor. Or, if he wanted them on display, in a glass jar.

Not that it was any of his business. "I'll take six." Longarm accepted the beer, slipped five of the cheroots into a pocket, and bit the twist off the sixth before striking a match and lighting the slender cigar.

The barman was right about the cheroots being fresh. The tobacco was moist and tasty, and Longarm drew the smoke deep into his lungs, let it out in a series of smoke rings that hung in the air overhead before dissipating, then reached for his mug of foaming beer.

"Do you have a deck o' cards I could have?" he asked.

Again the barman nodded. "For a nickel," the burly man said. "Hand them in when you're done, you get two cents back."

"All right." Longarm used a forefinger to shove a nickel from his change across the bar to the apron. The man pocketed the coin and bent to get a deck of pasteboards from somewhere below the bar.

The cards had been used before, but they were in decent condition, none of them marked or with corners bent.

"All right?" the barman asked.

"Fine," Longarm said. He stuck the cheroot between his

teeth, picked up his beer, and carried the beer and the deck of cards to one of the empty tables.

If someone came along who wanted to play a little low-stakes poker, that would be a fine way to pass the evening. Otherwise he would be content to play solitaire instead.

And either way he intended to keep his eyes and ears open.

Chapter 6

Longarm yawned and dealt five cards to each of the two gents who had joined him at the table and five to himself. The game was penny ante poker, something to pass the time, not to rake in any money.

"If you don't mind me askin'," he said as he studied the truly lousy hand he had dealt himself, "I'm new in town. What's it like here? Is there anybody a newcomer should walk soft around?"

The wheezing, red-faced man to his left acted annoyed by the questions. Apparently he wanted to concentrate on his hand. But the nicely dressed gentleman to Longarm's right tugged two cards out of the fan in his hand and pushed them to the center of the table.

"Two names you want to know," that gentleman said.

"Anything you need?" Longarm asked of the wheezer. That fellow was still studying what he had been dealt. Longarm turned his attention back to the fellow at his right. "Two names?"

The gent nodded. "Ira Collins and George Stepanek."

"An' they would be?" Longarm asked.

"Ira, he's the big he-coon around here. Owns half the buildings on Front Street and is working toward pulling in the other half. George is his . . . I suppose you would say that George is Ira's regulator. If you know the term."

"If you mean it like they use the word over in Wyoming," Longarm said, "then yeah. I know the term. It means George is a man to steer clear of if you want to stay outa trouble."

The gentleman nodded. "You have it right."

"One card," the wheezer said, finally deciding what he wanted to do with his hand. One card. Which meant that he had shit for cards and was relying on sheer luck. If he had asked for the lone card right away, it might have meant something, but the procrastination suggested he was on a fishing trip and had nothing to start with.

Longarm dealt the man his one card and two for the gentleman to his right. "Dealer stands pat," he said. He had nothing in his hand, but the stakes were agreeably low and the conversation was already paying off.

"Open for a quarter," the wheezer said, tossing a coin into the center of the table.

Trying to buy the tiny pot, Longarm thought. A quarter was a large bet in this game.

"I'll see your quarter and raise you fifty cents," the well-dressed gentleman returned.

"Too rich for me," Longarm said, tossing his cards into the discard pile.

"Your fifty cents and up a dollar," Wheezer said.

"And a dollar more," the gent responded.

Longarm sat back and watched while the two locals went at each other, building the pot until it was a respectable amount. When they finally got around to showing their hands, Wheezer turned out to have four treys, which he likely had

had to begin with. The man had simply been bluffing with that act of taking so much time to consider his cards. Longarm gave Wheezer a closer look.

He had underestimated the man to begin with. That was not a good way to begin this quest to help Helen.

Longarm waited until Wheezer had collected his winnings, then he raked the cards toward himself, made sure there was nothing but backs showing, and began to shuffle.

"Still straight draw poker," he mumbled as he shuffled. "Nothing wild. Penny to play."

He pushed his penny into the middle of the table and waited for the others to ante up before he once again began to deal.

Chapter 7

"Ira Collins. What can you tell me about him?" Longarm asked the waiter/cook and presumably the owner of the Tisbury Café the next morning.

"And who would you be?" the Tisbury counterman asked in return.

"Just a newcomer in town," Longarm said. "I heard the name last night over a friendly game of cards. Heard he was a big shot. So who is he? What does he do to swing such a wide loop?"

The local man polished some freshly washed platters but said nothing.

"Are you Tisbury?" Longarm asked.

"I am."

"An' this is your place."

Tisbury grunted. The man set a plate aside and threw his towel across a shoulder. "There's not much I can tell you. Mr. Collins, he owns this place."

"But I thought . . ."

"I started the business. Opened it six years ago when the

rails got here. Mr. Collins made me a generous offer. And I can still run the place. Mr. Collins pays me a nice salary too. It . . . it works out fine."

"If you say so," Longarm said. "But what can you tell me about Collins? Who is he? Where'd he come from?"

"I wouldn't know about any of that," Tisbury said, "and if I was you, I wouldn't be asking too many questions. You don't want to come to the attention of his man."

"That would be Stepanek," Longarm guessed.

"You've heard about him then."

"Only the name," Longarm said. "What can you tell me about him?"

"Mister, if you run into the man, you'll know it. He is . . . I probably could get in trouble myself for saying this, but he is one rough customer. Quick with his fists; quicker with his gun."

Longarm dragged his coffee cup closer and idly stirred the dark contents. "Maybe I should stay away from the gentleman then."

Tisbury grunted again. "Stepanek is no gentleman, but if you're lucky you won't ever find that out for yourself. And if anybody asks, you heard nothing from me. All right?"

"Agreed," Longarm said. "Anyway, it's true. I've heard nothing much from you about either fellow."

He laid a silver cartwheel down and said, "Thanks for the breakfast, Mr. Tisbury. Keep the change."

Longarm slid off the counter stool, hitched his britches up, and headed for the street.

Chapter 8

He wandered the streets to get acquainted with Helen's town. He thought of talking with her about Collins and Stepanek. She was really the person he needed to ask about them; she would not hold back in either her opinions or her descriptions. But this was not an appropriate hour to go visiting in a whorehouse.

At this early time of day only an employee or a very good friend was likely to be knocking at that particular door.

Better, he thought, to wait until this evening before he spoke with Helen again.

The time could be well spent, though, simply by walking. Later he could listen in on conversations in a saloon or two.

And of course this evening he would head for Helen's main whorehouse, where his comings or goings would simply be regarded as those of a horny traveler.

In the meantime he would . . .

"Bitch!"

The voice came from across the side street Longarm found himself on at the moment.

It seemed to be coming from inside a tailor's small shop. It was followed by the sound of a loud slap and a woman's voice crying out in pain.

Longarm was not fond of the idea of ladies being abused. Not even whores. And any lady in a tailor shop at this hour was not likely to be a whore.

He had not checked with Helen about the local habit—or laws—regarding when her girls were allowed to shop, but it was unlikely that any of the local whores would be up and about at this hour of the day anyway.

Curious, he angled across the street and entered the tailor shop, a bell rigged at the top of the door announcing his visit.

Inside he found a woman—he guessed her to be somewhere in her late thirties or early forties—behind the counter.

A tall, very lean man wearing a leather vest, black gloves, and a wide-brimmed pearl-gray hat stood at the end of the counter. The ivory grips of a pistol hung beneath his left armpit.

The left side of the woman's face was bright red and beginning to swell. A small trickle of blood seeped from the corner of her mouth.

And the man, who had obviously just hit the lady, had his hand drawn back ready to smack her again.

"Hello," Longarm said. He was smiling. Or at least his teeth were exposed. His eyes, however, had turned flinty, and any sensible human being would have known not to cross him right then. "Did I interrupt something?"

"Yes," the man growled.

"No, not at all," the lady said at the same moment.

"Get the fuck out of here," the man said.

"How may I help you, sir?" the lady asked.

Longarm approached the counter, still smiling. He took

his hat off and bobbed his head, just a customer ignorant of the tensions in the room, or so it seemed.

"I was thinking 'bout getting me some shirts made," Longarm said. "Nothin' fancy. Just one or two if the price ain't too dear."

"I said you'd best get the fuck out of here," the tall man snarled.

Longarm smiled at him. "And you'd best watch your mouth around this lady. You two aren't married, are you?"

The man just glared at him.

"No, sir, we are most definitely not married," the lady said.

"Mind what I said, sir," Longarm warned.

"Or what, asshole?"

"Or you and me will have us a learnin' session about how a man should act around ladies," Longarm answered.

"Do you know who I am?" the tall fellow snapped.

Longarm's phony smile became all the wider. "Don't know," he said. "Don't care."

"Get out, asshole, or we'll have that lesson for sure, right here and now."

Longarm bowed toward the lady. "My apologies, ma'am."

Then he turned and whipped his Stetson across the eyes of the tall and belligerent fellow.

Chapter 9

That got the ball rolling to a fare-thee-well. Before the tall man could react, Longarm dropped his hat and delivered a rapid-fire pair of blows to the fellow's gut.

The man doubled over, placing his face quite conveniently for an uppercut that pulped his nose and sent blood spraying onto some bolts of cloth stacked on a table nearby.

He staggered back, took a deep breath, and got himself set to enter the fray.

The fellow was quick. Longarm had to give him that. He came in like he knew what he was doing, light on his toes and moving from side to side. Longarm guessed the man had done some prizefighting somewhere in his past.

He feinted with a left but threw his right hand, hard and straight and quick. Longarm's forearm flicked it aside, and he hit the tall man in the face. Twice. Hard, quick, short jabs that did more damage to the already flattened nose and split the fellow's upper lip as well.

The man's upper body dipped to the side, and he landed a

punch that came out of nowhere and turned the left side of Longarm's face numb.

Bastard wasn't just nasty to women, Longarm realized. He could handle himself in a fight with a man too.

But then Longarm had had this sort of dance before.

He reared back and drove his right hand hard in an attempt to push the man's face into the back of his skull.

The punch was a powerful one. It sent the fellow staggering backward. He stopped, shook his head again, sending bright strings of blood onto the bolts of cloth around him . . . and sagged down onto his knees.

"All right, damn you," he muttered. "You s'prised me this time. You won't do that again, I fucking promise you."

The fellow grabbed hold of a table and pulled himself upright. Shook his head again and glared at Longarm. Then he stumbled to the door and out into the street.

Longarm watched him out of sight, cautious lest the fellow go for that ivory-handled shooter under his arm, but there was no return engagement and no firearms came into play.

Longarm turned to the lady and again bowed. "My apologies."

"No . . . I . . . thank you, sir." She picked up his Stetson, found a sponge on a shelf behind the counter, and used it to brush off Longarm's hat before handing it back to him. "George is . . . overly zealous at times, and he assumes more than I care to offer."

Longarm smiled. "Then I'm glad I happened by, miss."

"Did you really come in to see about shirts, sir?"

"No, ma'am. I heard you from out in the street. Don't like to intrude, but some things a gentleman doesn't do. Like hitting a lady, which I can plainly see that you are. I just hope he won't come back and take out on you what he couldn't do to me."

"Thank you for that thought too, sir." She stepped closer and went up onto tiptoes to examine the side of his face. "You're bleeding a little," she said. "Come into the back. I'll wash the blood off and do something about that cut."

Feeling was beginning to return to Longarm's face—the son of a bitch really could hit.

"That's mighty kind of you, ma'am."

"It is 'miss,' not 'ma'am,' and it is no trouble at all." She stepped to the door and turned the OPEN sign around to read CLOSED but did not bother turning the bolt to lock it. "This will only take a minute," she said. "Follow me, please."

Chapter 10

"It" took more than a minute. Considerably more. Dressing Longarm's cut led to coffee, which led to lunch, which led to an examination of his torso in case there might be damage there, which led to none-too-subtle suggestions that more clothing be removed, which led to . . .

"Ah, darlin', it feels mighty good to be inside that pretty body o' yours."

"If I had known how big your cock is, I would have had your clothes off before we wasted time having lunch."

"That wasn't a waste, ma'am. It just gave me more energy to spend bumpin' bellies with you now."

Iris Tyner laughed. And waggled her butt from side to side in response. Longarm happened to be deep inside her at the time. He rather liked the feel of it.

Iris was small, dark, and slim. She admitted to being thirty-eight years old, a statement that he suspected was the truth. And she liked to fuck.

"The problem," she had explained over lunch, "is that George seems to think one invitation to share my bed gives him proprietary rights over me anytime he wants more of the same. It doesn't. I may like sex . . . the fact is that I very much do like sex . . . but that does not make me his, or any man's, possession. I am an independent woman, not a whore. And certainly not a sex toy." She sighed. "George just doesn't understand that."

Now, the two of them entwined on Iris's narrow bed in the back room of her shop, Longarm shuddered and stiffened as a wad of sticky cum squirted deep inside the woman's slender body.

Iris had already reached her own climaxes at least three times, and those were only the ones Longarm was sure of. The way she grunted and moaned throughout made it a little difficult for him to tell when she was coming.

Iris was a girl who just plain liked to fuck, and she was not shy about letting the fact be known.

She was also not bad-looking. Unlike most women, Iris Tyner looked better naked than she did when she was dressed for the world to see.

She had small, nicely formed tits with pink nipples standing tall atop them, slender legs that could clamp around a man with remarkable strength, and a round, compact, lovely ass.

For some reason—he hoped it was not crabs—she kept her bush trimmed almost to the point of being shaved. It was unusual. But he liked it. The effect was a clean and quite lovely pussy.

With no hair to hide her private parts from view, her lips were pink and pretty. And her love hole gaped wet and ready as soon as she stepped out of her knickers.

Longarm finished and rolled off of her. He had to be careful about it because her bed was too narrow for them to sprawl. They lay pressed close together, Iris trailing her fingers over his now limp cock.

"Lovely," she said. She giggled. "There is something so pretty about a cock. Do you mind?"

"Mind what?"

"If I look a little closer?"

"Of course not. Whatever pleases you, darlin'."

Iris untangled herself from him and slid down toward the foot of the bed. "My, my," she mumbled.

She used a fingertip to lift his pecker, then peeled the foreskin back. She used thumb and forefinger to milk his dick, forcing a small pearl of white cum to the tip.

Iris's tongue flicked out, and she licked his juice away.

"Tasty," she said. "Would you mind . . . ?"

She did not wait for him to answer, just sucked his cock into her mouth.

"Careful what you're startin' there, darlin'," he warned.

Iris's answer was another giggle. And to suck him deeper into her mouth.

Longarm's response was immediate. And powerful. He came erect, strengthening and lengthening and filling Iris's mouth and on into her throat.

Her response was to mumble something that sounded very much like a cat's purring and to use her fingers to tickle his balls while she sucked.

This girl, he thought, was one helluva nice find.

Chapter 11

By the time Longarm got around to leaving Iris's bed, it was late in the afternoon, too late to accomplish much.

"Hungry?" Iris asked.

He nodded. And yawned. The day had been a strenuous one. In a very nice sort of way.

"I could cook something for us," Iris suggested.

He said, "If there's a nice place to eat in this town, I could take the two of us out to dinner." Longarm smiled. "I haven't had the pleasure of squiring a pretty lady in quite some time. If you're not ashamed to be seen on my arm, that is, me bein' a sort o' rough-hewn stranger here."

"I would be honored. And very pleased too, Custis. Get dressed while I find something I can gussy up with." She crawled over him to reach the floor. He stopped her halfway, and they nearly became sidetracked, but after a minute or two he took his tongue out of Iris's mouth and let her get off the bed.

Iris headed for a wardrobe at the side of the small, crowded room while Longarm stood and stretched for a moment, then reached for his hastily discarded clothing that was scattered hither and yon.

Five minutes later they were both dressed and ready to be seen in public.

"We can go out the front," Iris said. "The alley in back is always muddy because old man Barnes insists on watering his horse back there. The old fool pays a boy to carry buckets of water from the railroad's pump, and the kid can't handle a full bucket yet. He's a nice boy but too small for the job. Still, he does need the income. His ma is a railroad widow and doesn't have any sort of pension or anything to help her get along. I sell her yard goods as cheap as I can so I can try to help out a little."

Longarm followed the babbling little woman out into the shop, darker now that the sun was almost gone. He stopped her at the door and thoroughly kissed her before opening the door and escorting her out onto the public street.

He leaned down and whispered, "Where are we going?" He was supposed to be escorting her, but he had no idea where.

Iris laughed and said, "The Chauncey Hotel over on Second Street has the most elegant dining room in town. Can you afford something like that?"

"For the pleasure of the company of a beautiful lady like you, I reckon I can," he told her, bowing slightly as he did so.

Iris laughed again and hugged his arm. "Oh, I *am* glad you came along," she said.

They sauntered slowly toward the Chauncey, Iris telling him where to turn when need be, window-shopping along the way, and got there just about the time the sun disappeared below the horizon.

The front of the Chauncey was ablaze with lamplight, and inside was even brighter from the crystal-drop chandeliers hanging overhead. The waiters wore red jackets, and the tables were covered with white linen. The place settings looked like bone china, and the silverware appeared to be real silver.

"Like it?" Iris asked as she clung to the crook of his arm.

Longarm grinned down at her and said, "It's just the sort of place I'm used to." Then he laughed to admit to the lie. "Come on then. Let's go in an' put on the ol' feed bag."

Chapter 12

After dinner—a rather elegant affair indeed—Longarm walked Iris back to her shop. "Yes, I really live there. I can't afford to pay two rents out of what I make. Will you come inside?" she offered when they reached the front door.

"No, but I thank you. And I want to thank you for the pleasure of your company tonight." He winked and added, "And earlier too."

"Oh, that pleasure was mine," Iris said.

"I won't kiss you good night," Longarm told her. "Don't want folks to be gossiping."

Iris's answer was to throw her arms around Longarm's neck and plant a huge kiss on him, probing his mouth with her tongue.

He was tempted to change his mind and accompany the lady inside for a while, perhaps for the night, but that would not be accomplishing anything for Helen. He settled for the kiss, saw Iris indoors, and waited until her door was locked before he turned and walked toward Front Street, along the railroad.

The saloons—and there were plenty of them—were ablaze

with lights and music played on a piano. Longarm dropped in at several of the more likely-looking places and stayed only long enough to have a beer and eavesdrop on the conversations around him.

Most of the talk was uninteresting. Off-duty railroaders talked about bosses or coworkers. Cowhands talked about horses, both the good and the bad ones they had known. The miners seemed mostly to talk about the local whores.

Each group tended to gather in saloons that catered to their own sort. Longarm spent the bulk of his time sipping suds in the two saloons where the miners drank. He heard nothing there about the whorehouses, though, just the whores. He finished his brews and moved along.

In none of the saloons did he hear a word about Ira Collins. He did overhear one man grumbling about George Stepanek, but the man was drinking with a small group of friends and was disinclined to talk to a stranger.

Longarm made the rounds of all the town's watering holes until he was familiar with them and with their normal clientele. And until he was feeling more than a bit waterlogged by all the beer he had put behind his belt.

Time to head back to his hotel, he decided. While he could still navigate the way there.

He went outside, looked around a bit to get his bearings, then started walking back toward the Pickering and an empty hotel room.

He would have much preferred the acrobatics available in Iris's back room or the friendly company to be found in Helen's bedroom, but at the moment the Pickering seemed advisable.

He was a block away from the hotel when he heard a rush of feet coming fast behind him.

Coming much too fast.

Chapter 13

There were three of them, and they had bad intentions. Trying to roll him for his wallet, he assumed.

It was not a plan he intended to comply with.

Longarm spun to his right, lashing out with his knuckles extended into the throat of the first son of a bitch.

The man gagged and clutched his throat, dropping to his knees and puking into the dust and cinders of the street.

Behind him the second man avoided Longarm's punch by tripping over his downed partner. He did not, however, avoid the next punch. Longarm's fist split the bastard's lips and may well have loosened some teeth.

But there was a third . . .

Longarm more heard than felt the crunching blow onto the back of his head. The sound was like that of a pumpkin being thumped. Hollow and deep.

Deep inside his own skull.

It was something he found mildly interesting.

Something he intended to examine. When he got time.

For now, though, he would just lie there next to the man who was retching his guts out.

Interesting how he had gotten down there on the ground without really noticing. But there he was.

Longarm found that to be mildly funny.

He thought about laughing.

Thought about crying.

Thought about joining that other guy by puking up all that beer he had had during the evening.

Thought about . . . Fuck it. Thought about just going to sleep right there and then.

Longarm closed his eyes and let himself drift away into the gray void that was coming down to claim him.

Chapter 14

This hotel had one hard son-of-a-bitch of a bed. At the very least he wanted to change rooms. If all their beds were this lousy, he would change hotels.

Longarm cracked his eyes open.

And frowned.

The wall he was staring at was made of brick. He thought there was supposed to be wallpaper.

And in the other direction . . . there were bars.

He was in a jail cell. He could not remember why he would have been collared. He shook his head.

That was a mistake. The rapid motion made his head swim and his stomach do flip-flops. There was a distinct possibility that he was going to puke.

Longarm fought down that impulse and sat up on the edge of the jail bench. That helped. A little.

"Awake are you?" a voice came from the other side of the bars.

He thought, No, you asshole, I'm still sound asleep.

But aloud he said, "Yes, sir."

"Feeling better now?"

"Yes, sir, a little, thank you." Custis Long knew a bit about jailhouse etiquette and how a sensible man speaks to the fellow with the key. "Can I ask you a question?"

"Yeah, go ahead."

"What am I in for?"

The turnkey laughed. "You don't know?"

"No, sir, I don't." Longarm could learn to seriously dislike this son of a bitch. Wouldn't even have to work very hard at it. And, dammit, his head hurt.

"Drunk and disorderly. You was found passed out in the street. That's enough to earn you three days or three dollars, one or t'other."

"I wasn't passed out. Somebody beat me up," Longarm said.

"Sonny, do you have any idea how many times I've heard that one?" the jailer responded. The man walked into view and Longarm got a look at him. The turnkey was a scrawny little son of a bitch with a shaggy beard and nearly bald dome. His hair, both head and beard, had the washed-out sort of white that once had been red. He wore bib overalls and eyeglasses.

"Did I have my wallet when you picked me up?" Longarm asked.

"I didn't look into your pockets, sonny, but I noticed the right front in your britches was turned inside out," the jailer said.

That was a relief, Longarm thought. The thieves had gotten some money from him, but his credentials as a deputy U. S. marshal were intact. The money could easily be replaced. The badge could not.

There would be no point in making a police report about the attack, he knew. This was a railroad town. Half a dozen trains could have come and gone while he lay unconscious in this jail cell, and the three men who jumped him could have gotten onto any one of them.

For that matter, dark as it had been, he was not really sure he could describe the trio. Or recognize them if he saw them again.

But he wished he could get his hands on the asshole who'd bashed him from behind. It was a favor he would be pleased to return.

"What about my Colt?" he asked.

"Yeah, you was wearing that. It's out here in the desk. You can have it back when you get out."

Longarm blinked a little and took inventory of himself. The back of his head felt like it had been caved in. But he knew it hadn't been. There was some matted blood back there that he would wash out once he was free to do so. The damage could have been much worse. Likely his Stetson had cushioned some of the blow.

His wallet was in an inside coat pocket. That, including the badge it contained, would go into the hotel safe as soon as he got back there.

The leather also contained some currency. The thieves had missed finding that. But then hard money, coins, was the most common. A good many men simply did not trust paper money. The thieves had not been looking for paper, just for metal. Thank goodness.

"Mister. Sir. Did you say I can get out if I pay a fine of three dollars?"

"That's right. Three dollars or three days, whatever you like."

"I'll pay the three dollars," Longarm said.

"Cash money? We don't take no jawbone here."

"Cash money," Longarm assured him.

"Give me a minute to get my keys then, and I'll let you out."

Longarm stood. He felt wobbly and a little nauseous, but that would pass. Right now what he wanted was to get out of this cell, get back to the hotel, and clean up. He needed to send his clothes out to be cleaned too.

And he needed to see Helen again.

Come to think of it, his wallet would probably be safer with her than with some hotel clerk who might very well have sticky fingers to finish the job those robbers had started.

The jailer reappeared, carrying a steel ring with half a dozen keys attached. The only key Longarm was interested in was the one to this cell. The man found it on the second try, and Longarm was a free man again.

Chapter 15

"Send a boy up to my room, would you. I need to have some clothes dry cleaned."

The desk clerk at the Pickering nodded and yawned.

"And if you don't mind, what time is it?" Longarm asked.

The clerk pointed toward the wall-hung regulator clock to the right of the hotel desk. It was only nine-thirty in the morning, much too early to be seen calling on Helen.

"Thanks." Longarm wearily climbed the stairs and let himself into his room. He barely had time to strip off his clothes before the boy showed up at his door to collect them.

"I'm sorry, but I forgot to mention to the clerk, I need a tub and some bathwater too. And soap. I didn't bring my own."

"All right, sir. I won't be long with your water. The tub is in the closet just down the hall there." The boy pointed and left, carrying Longarm's filthy clothes wadded into a bundle.

Longarm wrapped a towel around his waist and trudged down the hall to locate the copper tub and drag it back to his room. By the time he was done with that, the boy was back with the first two buckets of water hot from a reservoir downstairs.

There was barely enough to cover his butt, but he sank down into it with a loud sigh. The heat felt mighty good on his battered body. He scooped some water up with his hands and spilled it over his head. He used a dab of soft soap to cleanse the dried blood that was caked in the hair on the back of his head, then used more to bathe his face and wash under his arms and in his crotch.

The kid came back with two more buckets.

"Just pour those over me, boy."

"The water is pretty hot, sir."

"That's all right. It feels good."

"Yes, sir."

Damn kid was right. The water felt like surely it must be close to boiling. No matter. Longarm let the heat soak into his bones. If this kept up, he thought, he might get to feeling human in another half hour or so.

"Boy, hand me that wallet you see laying on the bureau there."

"Yes, sir."

Longarm took the wallet and extracted a dollar bill. He handed it to the kid.

"I don't have any change, sir, but I can run downstairs and get some."

"I don't want no change back, son. You earned it."

The boy's eyes went wide. "The whole dollar, sir?"

Longarm nodded and closed his eyes for a moment, then opened them again. "One more thing before you go, please."

"Yes, sir. Anything you want, sir."

"Hand me one o' them cigars you'll see over there. And a match."

Longarm fired up a cheroot, thanked the kid again, then

slid as far down in the warm water as he could get, his cigar leaving a stream of smoke hanging above the tub.

He relaxed and let the warmth soothe his aching muscles. He had forgotten to grab the towel out of the wardrobe and would likely half freeze when he got out of the tub and the air reached his wet skin, but no matter. There would be time enough to worry about that when it happened.

Right now all he wanted was to stay where he was and soak. Later on he could think about something to eat. Maybe a shot or two of rye whiskey.

And this evening he would be like any customer with a hard-on and a little money to spend and go visit with Helen at her place.

Chapter 16

Longarm slept the afternoon away, then got up and dressed in his spare clothing. It was good to feel clean and dry and reasonably well rested again. He went downstairs and turned his key in at the desk, then walked over to Tisbury's for a steak, fried, and potatoes, also fried, and a slab of dried apple pie, all of it very good stuff.

After supper he made his way over to Helen's whorehouse. Her ladies were pretty, but they were not tempting. Given the choice he would have rather been with Iris than with any of these working girls, no matter how pretty they were.

If, that is, Iris would have him. She had made it abundantly clear that one romp in her bed did not give a gent a free pass for future pleasures.

Right now, though . . .

"Is Miss Helen here?" he asked the girl who answered the door. He had forgotten to ask Helen if she was using her real name, so he was not sure if he should ask for Helen Morrow or . . . who knew what else.

"Have a seat in the parlor, sir. I'll see if she is available. Your name, please?"

"Custis," Longarm said. "She knows me."

"Yes, sir." The girl bobbed her head and headed for the back of the house. Longarm entered the parlor and settled onto an overstuffed chair.

The bevy of whores preened and postured, vying in their own fashion to be the one the tall gentleman chose. The room smelled of perfume and powders. The girls were pink and many of them plump, with plenty of tit for a man to play with, and their gowns made the most of what they had to offer, barely covering the essentials.

The girl who had greeted him returned quickly. "Miss Helen said you are to go right back, sir. Do you know the way?"

"Yes, thank you." Longarm headed down the hallway toward the back of the house. He stopped at Helen's door and knocked.

"Custis? I'm glad to see you, dear," Helen said, opening the door and ushering him inside. "Can I get you something? Are you hungry?"

"I'm fine. Just ate, thanks. But about that rye . . . ?"

She laughed and took him by the elbow, leading him into her office and living quarters and seating him in a comfortable armchair. That was followed with a generous measure of her excellent rye whiskey. "Now," she said. "Tell me what you have learned."

Chapter 17

"Do you think you are making any progress?" Helen asked after Longarm had brought her up to date with the little he had learned so far.

Longarm shrugged and took a small sip of the superior rye whiskey. "It's too soon to tell, darlin'. Something like this, 'bout all a man can do is to throw some chum in the water an' let it float. Maybe something will turn up, maybe not."

"You aren't giving up, are you?" Helen sounded worried.

"Course not. I'm just getting started." Longarm set his whiskey aside and reached for a cheroot. Helen quickly struck a match for him and held the flame to the end of the cigar. "Thanks," he said and leaned back to pick up the whiskey glass again.

"What can I do for you?" she asked. Before he had a chance to answer, Helen said, "One thing I insist on doing is replacing the money those robbers stole from you. How much was it?"

Longarm shook his head. "That don't matter. Wasn't none o' your fault."

"Of course it matters, dear. You would not have been here if it weren't for me and my problems. Besides, I want to."

"It's all right, I tell you," he insisted.

"It isn't all right. And you wouldn't believe how much I make with these houses. I can certainly afford it. Now, how much was it? Three hundred? Four?"

Longarm laughed. "Darlin', you've got an inflated idea of how much money a deputy marshal makes and is apt to have in his pockets."

"A hundred then." Helen got up, opened a drawer in her rolltop desk, and pulled out a handful of gold coins in the smaller values. Without bothering to count them, she dropped the gleaming disks into Longarm's shirt pocket. "And don't you say a word about not taking that," she said. "As it is I owe you more than I could possibly pay, just for you coming here to help me. So shut your mouth, sonny, and do as you're told." But she was laughing when she added that last part.

Longarm shut his mouth. And reached for the rye.

"Do you know what you want to do next?" she asked.

He nodded. "I think I'm gonna open me a saloon." Then, a twinkle in his eye, he added, "An' maybe run me some whores of my own."

"Collins won't let you do either of those without his blessing," Helen said.

Longarm chuckled and said, "Exactly," emphasizing the word with a string of smoke rings that drifted toward the ceiling before they dissipated into the perfumed air.

Chapter 18

"I almost forgot," Helen said.

"Mm?"

"You said you wanted to know if any more of those letters came?"

"That's right."

"There were three more in the box today," Helen said.

"Did you save them for me?"

She once again left her chair and crossed heavily over to the rolltop. From one of the pigeonholes she produced an envelope. The glue on the envelope flap had been carefully opened—steam, Longarm guessed—and the note inside exposed.

"There were three, but they were all the same," Helen said. "I burned the other two, but I saved this one to show to you." She handed the opened envelope to him.

Longarm pulled the note out.

I KNOW YOU, SARAH. I KNOW YOUR PARENTS.
DO THEY KNOW WHAT YOU DO HERE? I CAN TELL

THEM. YOU KNOW, THIS MAY BE A GOOD TIME FOR YOU TO TAKE A TRIP—A LONG TRIP, IF YOU KNOW WHAT I MEAN. THINK ABOUT THAT, SARAH. THINK ABOUT IT. TELL THE OLD BITCH YOU WANT TO GO HOME. THE TRAIN WILL TAKE YOU RIGHT THERE, SARAH

Longarm read the note twice, then said, "You say they were all the same?"

Helen nodded. "Except for the names, yes. Sarah is the girl who works under the name Daisy. She's a good girl. All the gentlemen like her."

"I wonder why three letters," Longarm said.

"There was one addressed to a girl at each of my houses if that means anything."

"Whoever is doing this is trying to ruin you," Longarm mused.

"The son of a bitch could do it too if any of these letters got through. My girls are spooked enough without this."

Longarm raised an eyebrow. "Spooked how?"

"Out at the hog ranch someone has started riding up in the middle of the night and yelling. Shouting ugly things. Some of the girls . . . they aren't very bright, you know, even the not so pretty ones . . . some of the girls have decided there are haunts and goblins out there. I lost another girl just today. A lovely little Mexican thing. She came to me crying and clutching at her rosary. She said she was afraid of the ghosts of all the men she has been with. Not that the johns are dead. She is afraid of them anyway. She took an afternoon train south."

"I want to meet this Collins fellow," Longarm said. "You think he's the one behind your troubles?"

"He almost has to be," Helen said. "But be careful when you meet him. You don't want to cross Stepanek."

Longarm grinned. "You got that wrong, darlin'. It's Stepanek that oughta be careful not to cross me."

Helen laughed, then got up and said, "Let me refresh your glass, sweetie."

Chapter 19

Longarm woke early the next morning. He shaved carefully and used a splash of the smell-good stuff that a woman back in Denver had given him. While he was busy doing that, he sent a bellboy out to collect his clean clothes from the dry cleaner—who'd done a good job, not perfect but good—and freshly black his boots.

He went from the hotel to Tisbury's for breakfast, then over to the barber's for a quick trim.

"Who should I see about finding a place in town to rent?" he asked the barber who was working on him.

"Like a house, you mean?" the barber asked.

"No, like a storefront. I'm thinking this might be a likely place to open a saloon," Longarm said.

"Oh, now, that's different. For commercial property there's only one person you want to talk to," the barber told him. "Go see Mr. Collins. He doesn't own quite all the property in town, but he owns all of it that's available."

"You're sure of that?"

"Yes, sir. Positive," the barber said.

"Where would I find this Mr., er, Collins, did you say?"

The barber stopped snipping and pointed. "You just go . . ."

Half an hour later Longarm stood on the sidewalk outside Western Land and Investments. He admired the sign for a moment, then took a deep breath and opened the door.

The first person he saw when he stepped inside was the tall man named George with whom he'd fought inside Iris's seamstress shop.

The fellow named George was George Stepanek, it seemed.

And the two men who were idling in the outer office looked vaguely familiar too. They could have been two of the three who jumped him on the street, although he was not sure about that.

Stepanek, though . . . he was sure about Stepanek.

"Hello, Georgie," Longarm said with a grin as he removed his Stetson. "How're you feeling today, Georgie?"

Stepanek looked like he positively itched to go for that ivory-handled revolver that hung under his left armpit.

But he swallowed back the impulse and said, "What do you want here, mister?"

"Business," Longarm said. "But not with you. I want to see Mr. Collins."

"Wait here. I'll ask if he wants to see you," Stepanek growled. The man whirled and disappeared into a hallway leading toward the back of the offices.

Chapter 20

Ira Collins was a surprise. The man was trim, fit, heavily muscled . . . and not much more than five feet tall. He had dark hair and a spade beard and was wearing a handsomely tailored suit on his tiny frame. Even from within the suit coat, though, his biceps were obvious, so much so that his arms hung a little apart from his body. Like those of an ape, Longarm thought. But the reason in Collins's case was that his upper body was so muscular that his arms could not hang close to his body.

He had another surprise to deliver when Longarm stood before him.

"Greetings, Custis Long from Denver," the little man said.

"You've been checking up on me," Longarm said.

"Of course," Collins replied. "You appeared like Galahad to rescue the fair maiden." He smiled. "And quite thoroughly thrashed my man Stepanek in the process. Then you squired said maiden to a luxurious dinner and spent the ensuing night with her." Collins laughed. "There is much about you to interest a man, Mr. Long. But the really important information is lacking. Who are you, Mr. Long? What do you want here?"

"There isn't much 'bout me that would interest you," Longarm drawled. "I'm just a fella tryin' to get along in the world."

"And the nature of your business with me today?"

"I'm thinkin' about opening a saloon. Just a small outfit. Maybe put in a few poker tables. Buy me a few girls since I know a fella down in Denver that will sell for a fair price."

Collins paused for a long moment, pulling at his beard and frowning. "Somehow, Mr. Long, you do not appear to be the sort of man who would be content with operating a saloon. In fact, you might be a threat to me if you enter business here. You might become . . . greedy. You might want it all." He smiled . . . if the expression could be called that. "And in this town, I have it all. And I intend to keep it too."

"I'm no threat. Just a fella who wants to do a little business," Longarm assured him.

"I am not so sure," Collins said.

"Oh, I'm sure you'd have your people keep a close eye on me to make sure I ain't no threat."

"You could count on that, Mr. Long."

"Good. Send 'em in in droves." Longarm laughed. "Just make sure they buy some drinks while they're there. They'll all be welcome."

"Even George?"

"Ha." Longarm nodded. "Sure. Even Stepanek. Tell him he's welcome anytime. But to mind his manners."

"I shall tell him," Collins said.

" 'Shall,' " Longarm repeated. "Does that mean we can do some business?"

"Possibly. You are looking for a business location?"

"That's right. Not too big. Decent location. That'd be important."

"I have two properties that might suit," Collins said. "George will take you to look at them. You should know, however, that my terms are not negotiable. Your rent will be forty percent of your trade. One of my people will audit your books to verify the amount. And mind you, that is forty percent of your gross."

"I'll agree to forty percent," Longarm said, "but of the net profit, not off the gross income. Unlike you, I have a stiff cost of doing business. Gotta lay out for product an' so on. I might be able to live payin' forty percent off the profit but not off the gross."

"I told you my terms are not negotiable," Collins said.

Longarm extended his hand to the man. "Then I thank you for your time, sir, an' I'll be movin' along to another town."

Collins seemed surprised. He took Longarm's hand and shook it automatically but acted like he scarcely was aware of the gesture.

Longarm turned and started for the door.

"Wait," Collins barked before Longarm got out. "Come back here. I think we can talk."

Longarm turned, but without walking back toward the little man's desk he said, "Off the profit?"

Collins nodded. "Off the profit," he agreed.

"I'll tell Stepanek you need to see him. Then he and I can go look at those two locations. He can let you know which one I'll be takin'."

Chapter 21

It was no contest. One of the vacancies was half a block from the railroad depot, the other a corner location three blocks distant.

"I'll take the corner," Longarm said to the scowling George Stepanek.

"Really? The other is closer to the trains."

"It ain't necessarily the train passengers that I'm lookin' for," Longarm told him.

Stepanek shrugged and handed Longarm a key. Then he walked away, tossing "I'll tell Collins" over his shoulder.

Longarm stepped inside his newly acquired property. The place was about fifteen feet wide by forty deep and was bare to the walls and floor. It needed . . . everything.

He stood there in the empty place, looking at the dust motes floating in the air. Then he threw his head back and broke into laughter. A saloonkeeper. A businessman. Him. If that wasn't enough to get a man's belly to jiggling, nothing should be.

He walked back and forth through the store, looking and planning. After a half hour he left, locking up behind him.

"This is good whiskey," Longarm observed, holding up his glass to inspect the color of the liquor. "Where d'you get it?"

Helen Morrow snorted and told him, "Never you mind where I get it. I'll send you a couple bottles for your own pleasure, but you are not going to stock it. It costs too much. You'll buy medium-quality liquors, first-rate beer. And you will make a profit.

"You need to start thinking like a businessman, Custis, not as a fellow reveler. What's more, when it comes to the hard stuff, you need to stock at least three levels of quality. You serve the best for the first two shots. No more. Then the middling stuff. If the customer keeps drinking after two or three of those, you can safely shift to the cheap horse piss; he won't be able to tell the difference by then anyway."

"Dammit, Helen, that sounds like cheating," Longarm protested.

"Not at all," Helen said. "The man orders a drink. That is what he gets. If he orders a shot of your best, give him that. But he won't. Not one time in a hundred." She smiled and leaned forward to pat him on the cheek. "Business, Custis. You have to think of profitability in the smallest detail. In everything you do. Everything."

The thought of that local saloon charging for the use of an already used deck of cards came to mind. It was only pennies, but it was profit. "I . . . think I see what you mean, darlin'."

"And don't ever forget, dear, it is my money that is at risk here, not yours."

He smiled. "And in the end it's you that will have another established saloon where you can pick up that trade an' maybe run some o' your girls at the same time."

"Why, Custis," Helen said, batting her eyelashes in mock surprise, "what a lovely thought. Now, why didn't I think of that!"

Longarm laughed and took a small swallow of the truly excellent rye whiskey. Which he would *not* be stocking behind his own bar when the . . . What should he call the place? Then he laughed again. "The Star," he said aloud.

"What?"

"The Star," Longarm repeated. "I'm gonna name the place the Star Saloon." He grinned. "Kinda fits, don't you think, for a deputy marshal's place?"

Helen threw her head back and roared with laughter, her large body shaking.

"Mind if I have another o' this good stuff?" Longarm asked, leaning forward for the bottle. "Now, where'd you say I can get my wet goods? And what about carpenters? Who would you recommend there? And how the hell is a boss supposed to act anyway?" He shook his head. "This is all confusing to an innocent country boy like me, darlin'."

"You will learn, Custis. It may be in fits and starts, a bit at a time, but you will certainly learn."

Chapter 22

"A man needs a place to prop his foot," Longarm explained to one of his carpenters, "but it doesn't have to be a brass rail. Brass rails cost a bundle. Believe me, I know. I looked into buyin' one. Damn things come dear. So in the Star we'll build a . . . like a step or a little shelf at the front o' the bar, down at floor level, where a man can rest a boot while he's propped himself up on the bar. D'you see what I mean, James?"

"Yes, sir, I do. How high do you want it?"

Longarm pondered that for a moment, thinking back to all the rails he had propped himself up on in one saloon or another. Finally he held his two hands apart and said, "'Bout this tall, James. You measure it out, but make it about so high."

"Yes, sir."

"Mister." A scrawny, rat-faced little man tugged at his sleeve.

"I'm busy," Longarm snapped. This saloon proprietor shit was already wearing thin. And they were still days, if not weeks, away from opening.

"Yes, and I'm going to dump your barrels of beer in the damn street if you can't take time to tell me where to put them," the little man snapped right back at him.

"What? Beer? It's here already? I . . . Give me a minute. I have to clear space for them along the wall there." Raising his voice, he shouted, "Tommy, do you have the cradles ready to take the beer barrels? Get them ready because the beer is here and it has to go somewhere." Turning back to the little man, he pointed. "Over there."

The freighter grunted, nodded, and went on his way to get Longarm's beer delivered.

The Star was beginning to smell like sawdust, not a speck of which was being thrown away or burned. It, and more, was needed to cover the floor several inches deep.

And the cuspidors. Where the hell were those cuspidors that he ordered?

The card tables were built and stacked along the side wall to keep them out of the way. And stools. It was cheaper and easier to build stools than chairs, so the Star would be known for its stools.

No mirror on the back wall. Not yet. It remained to be seen what sort of clientele the Star would attract, and a rowdy crowd could become damned expensive if they broke an actual mirror. Longarm settled for polished steel instead of glass. Polished steel and a dartboard shaped like a buxom woman. He could just guess where the majority of the darts would be aimed. Not landed, necessarily, but aimed.

"Where . . . ?"

"Back there," Longarm answered before the man could finish his sentence. "By the back door. Just stack the crates there for now. I'll break 'em down and put everything away when the bar an' the cabinets are finished."

"How about . . . ?"

"Over there, I think," he said, pointing.

"Mister. Hey, mister."

Longarm turned. Questioned. Directed. Fumed and worried. This shit about being a businessman was no walk in the damn park, he was discovering.

But the place was slowly taking shape.

If they didn't watch out, the Star was going to start looking like a proper saloon.

Longarm paused to reach for a cheroot. Lighted it. He took in a deep breath and slowly let it out.

Helen's money and his time were combining to turn into something here.

But so far there was no indication of the troubles that had been plaguing her and her girls.

Chapter 23

"Drink up, boys. First drink is free. But you," he pointed, smiling, "I seen you take two o' them free 'first' drinks already. So pay for the next one, will you, or I'll be broke an' out of business in my first week." Laughing, he raised his voice, "Welcome to the Star, boys. Drink up an' be merry."

A pair of musicians, a banjo player and a fiddler, twanged away from a makeshift stage constructed of empty packing crates that had once held glass mugs and shot glasses.

The place was packed with a mixture of townspeople and passersby, all attracted by the lure of free beer and cheap whiskey.

For this opening night only, Longarm—or his bartender Robert, to be more accurate—was pouring a decent, but cheap, brand of keg whiskey for a nickel, while the beer was for the most part free.

That was probably not good business, he conceded, but then his purpose with the Star was not to make money but to call Ira Collins's and George Stepanek's hand.

Thinking of whom, he saw Stepanek's hat floating above

the crowd as the tall enforcer came into the newly opened saloon.

Longarm pushed his way through the throng until he was facing Stepanek. "Something you want, George? A beer? Would you rather have a whiskey? Bar whiskey here is rye, but I have bourbon, tequila, and brandy if you prefer. What will you have?"

Stepanek glared at him but did not answer. Collins's man looked over the crowd for several long moments, then turned and made his way back outside. Longarm followed him.

He buttonholed Stepanek and took him by the lapel before the man could slither away. Longarm brushed an imaginary speck of lint away but held on to the coat much longer than was necessary, delivering a message of sorts to Stepanek.

"No need for you to check things over, George," Longarm said. "Besides, I'm sure that accountant who's handling my books is reporting back to Collins quicker'n he tells me anything. So unless you want to put down some money on the bar, from now on you stay the fuck outa my place." He smiled a crocodile smile. "Or I'll whup your ass again, just like I did that day in Iris's place."

"You son of a—"

Before Stepanek could get the rest out, Longarm had a powerful grip on the wrist of the man's gun hand with his own left, while his right curled around the Adam's apple in George Stepanek's throat.

"Careful what you do or say, George," Longarm warned. "I whupped you that first time, I can do it again. Next time I might break something. What good would you be to Collins with the fingers o' your gun hand all busted to shit?"

"You bastard," Stepanek hissed. "You only beat me that time because you surprised me. I could take you. I will take you. Just as soon as Mr. Collins gives me leave to break you in two." He took a deep breath. "Something else you should think about. I'm better than you with a gun. I'm the best there is with a pistol. Think about that."

Longarm laughed. "Could be we'll have to find out about that someday, George. But not tonight, I'm thinking." He took his hand away from Stepanek's throat and let go of the man's gun hand as well. Longarm stepped back a pace, his right hand fiddling with his belt buckle—conveniently near the butt of his .45.

Stepanek glanced down and gauged the distance between Longarm's fingers and the grips of the Colt. "No. Not tonight," he said. "But . . . sometime."

"Sure, George. Sometime. Meanwhile I'll go back inside an' tremble in fear." Longarm laughed again. That infuriated Stepanek. As it was intended to.

"Bastard."

"Tell that to Mr. Collins. Meanwhile, stay the fuck away from me or I might forget my manners an' hurt you," Longarm said.

Deliberately he turned his back on George Stepanek and went back inside the Star.

Chapter 24

It was an interesting thing, what liquor did to some men. To the point that Longarm was thinking it was rougher being a saloonkeeper than being a deputy United States marshal.

So far this Saturday evening he had had to break up three fistfights and summon his swamper, old Johnny Mayfield, to clean up two puddles of puke, the second one made all the worse by the huge quantity of Mexican chuck the sickly man had just consumed.

It was rougher, Longarm concluded, and smellier too.

And so far he did not seem to be a whit closer to fixing Helen's problem with Ira Collins.

But he was learning a hell of a lot about the town and its people just by wandering through the saloon during working hours.

"Are you all right, Custis?" Helen asked.

They sat, as usual, in her quarters downstairs in the best among her whorehouses. It was late, and Longarm had turned the place over to Robert Ware, whom he was beginning to think of as his lifeline to sanity. Robert was bartender, assistant boss, and font of knowledge when it came to both the booze and the effects the stuff had on human beings.

The Star would remain open all night tonight. Robert would hand off to the night manager at midnight.

He yawned and scratched his left side. He had not been getting much in the way of sleep since he became an independent businessman. "I'd best be getting back," he said. "I want to see how well Bucky Doyle can handle things."

"If Robert says he can do it, then he can do it," Helen offered.

"Yeah, I know that, but . . ."

"Relax, Custis. If you insist on going back, at least get some rest. You look wound up tight as a nun's twat. Go home. Fuck one of your girls."

"Your girls, you mean," Longarm said.

Helen laughed. "They're yours at the moment, dear. I picked good ones, just for you."

"They seem like good ones," Longarm said.

"But for Pete's sake, don't spoil them," Helen said. "You'll ruin them for me if you give them too much of what they make. I heard you were talking about giving them more than the half they're entitled to." She pointed a plump forefinger at him. "Give a whore more than that and she gets greedy. She'll be expecting that much everywhere she works, and that just isn't going to happen. Keep that up and I'll have to fire girls and buy new ones. That or have them professionally beaten to get them back in line."

Longarm raised an eyebrow. "Professionally beaten? What the hell is that?"

"Just what I said. It's a beating given by a man who is an expert on the female body and with the infliction of pain. Believe me, a girl who has been worked over by a professional won't want to go through it a second time. It leaves her . . . eager to please, you might say."

"And you would do that to them?"

"If I must in order to keep them in line. Of course."

"There are times, Helen, when you really surprise me."

"Stay in business for a little while, Custis, and you will learn to agree with me. Believe me, being a lawman is nothing compared with being a saloonkeeper."

"I believe you, darlin'," he said. He wanted Helen to feel that her investment in the Star was in good hands.

When he got back to his saloon a half hour later, he suspected more than ever that what she'd said was right.

Chapter 25

A stocky little son of a bitch, whose clothes suggested he was one of the miners, had another man, a cowboy, backed up against the bar with the muzzle of a revolver in his face.

The cowboy had a pistol of his own in a holster dangling from his belt, but a gun wrapped in leather is no match for one in the hand.

The miner's pistol was cocked, Longarm could see.

And the cowboy was so pale with fear that he looked like he was dead already.

"D-d-d-d-don't." He quivered. "D-don't shoot."

"And don't you be calling me names," the miner growled.

"I d-d-didn't mean nothing," the cowboy insisted.

The miner waved his pistol a few inches from the nose of the offending cowboy. The little man had every appearance of someone who had been pushed just a little too far and was now intent on doing something about it. Something very drastic. Something quite possibly lethal.

"P-p-p-please," the lanky cowboy moaned.

The fellow might have been tip-top with cows and horses.

Longarm had no way to tell that. But he was damn sure no hero when it came to firearms. Longarm could see that in the dark, wet stain that was spreading down his left leg. The man had pissed himself.

Feeling more than a little disgusted, Longarm strode across the saloon floor to the little miner.

"Put it away," he snarled, his voice cold.

"He called me—"

"I don't give a shit what he called you, mister, but I know I don't want you to shoot the son of a bitch here in my place. Get blood an' brains all over the floor. Run people out o' here when they're in a mood to buy more drinks. You'd cause me to lose business, an' I can't have that. You understand? Now, put the damn gun away."

Longarm reached out and took hold of the barrel of the miner's pistol. He slipped his little finger in between the hammer and the frame of the revolver so it could not discharge even if the miner was idiot enough to pull the trigger.

Then he twisted, plucking the gun out of the hand of the distraught man.

The cowboy's knees sagged once he was no longer in danger. He collapsed back against the bar behind him and looked like he was close to breaking out in tears.

"Thank . . . thank you."

"I'm gonna give you some advice, sonny. Take that shooter off your hip. Give it away, sell it, whatever the fuck you like, but get rid of it. You don't have the temperament to wear a gun. It'll just get you in trouble. An' mind your tongue while you're at it. You oughtn't to go around insulting people, or the next man you offend might just go ahead an' shoot."

"But all I said was—"

"I don't give a fat crap what you said, mister. I don't want to hear it. Now, the both o' you go home. You've had enough to drink." He turned to the miner. "You. I'm gonna put this gun o' yours behind the bar there. You can get it back tomorrow."

"I'm not drunk," the miner insisted.

"No, if you was drunk you probably would've pulled the trigger, an' then you would've been in for hanging. Or thirty years behind bars. Either way you'd've been damn unhappy come morning. Now, get the hell out o' here."

The cowboy had already skedaddled, slipping out practically at a run while Longarm was busy with the miner.

"Go on now," Longarm barked.

The little miner got. But slower and with more dignity than the cowboy had displayed.

Longarm sighed. He let the hammer of the miner's pistol down to safe cock, then handed the gun across the bar to Bucky.

Chapter 26

Longarm handed the keys off to Robert to handle for the rest of the evening.

He turned, took Iris Tyner into his arms, and kissed the lady most thoroughly. "Is it just me, or are you getting prettier every day?"

"Flatterer," she said, laughing. "I know why you are saying sweet things to me. You just want to get into my pants."

"Of course I do," he said. "And is there anything wrong with that?"

Iris pretended to ponder the question for a moment, then shook her head and said, "No, now that I think about it. There isn't a thing wrong with it. In fact, I'm hoping you will."

"Will what?" he teased.

"Will fuck my brains out," Iris said.

"Well I certainly intend to give it my best shot, ma'am." He swept her up off the floor—she seemed to weigh next to nothing, but then she was a very small girl—and carried her into her quarters in the back of her shop.

It took only a few moments more for the two of them to get their clothes off.

"Damn, you look good, lady," Longarm said, smiling.

"Why, thank you most kindly, sir. May I say that you are not exactly unpleasant to look at yourself."

Longarm wrapped his arms around her and kissed her again, then picked her up and placed her onto her cot.

"One thing," he said. "You got to get a bigger bed for this place. Or take on smaller lovers. One or the other." He winced and rubbed the top of his head where he had just bumped it on the wall at the head of her bed.

Iris laughed and said, "Here, let me kiss the spot."

"It's down here," Longarm said, directing her attention to a very erect cock.

"You liar," she giggled. "I saw what you bumped, and it wasn't that."

"True," he agreed, "but bumps up here tend to come out down there. So down there is where it needs to be kissed if you really want to make it well."

"I certainly want to make it better," she said, "so I suppose I ought to . . ." She completed the thought by wriggling down to his waist level and taking his prick into her hand.

"I thought you said you were gonna kiss it," Longarm said.

"I did. And I will. Now, shut up and let me admire this thing of yours for a minute, will you?"

"Yes, ma'am."

Iris contemplated his cock for a long moment. She rose to her knees and reached to turn up the wick on the wall lamp overhead, then returned to the subject at hand. She peeled his foreskin back, then leaned forward and took the head of his cock between her lips.

She licked him thoroughly, running her tongue around the

head then down into the folds of skin that had been pushed below the red, engorged glans.

"If you knew how that feels . . . ," he said.

Iris did not answer except by taking him into her mouth. She had a rather small mouth. But a talented and accepting throat.

"Oh, jeez," he mumbled as his cock pushed past the tight constriction at the back of her mouth and on into her throat.

As big as he was, Iris was able to take all of him into her mouth. She gagged only a little and only at first. After that she moved up and down on him, slowly at first but then soon accelerating the pace, until he had to reach out and put a hand on the back of her pretty head to stop her.

Iris looked up, his dick still lodged deep inside her mouth. She lifted her eyebrows in inquiry.

"You'd best leave it be," he answered the unspoken question, "unless you want me to spray your tonsils with a load o' cum, lady. And it's only fair to tell you that it's been a while since I was able to unload that thing, an' my balls are awful full."

The corners of Iris's eyes crinkled with silent laughter.

And she went back to riding him, pushing him deep into her throat and back out to her mouth, over and over, faster and faster.

"I warned you," Longarm mumbled.

And shot his load into Iris's throat.

Chapter 27

"You're a darlin'," he mumbled as he nuzzled Iris's ear.

"And you're a stud," she responded.

Longarm kissed her and worked his way lower, taking first one nipple and then the other between his lips, sucking and licking as Iris wriggled beneath his touch.

"Yes," she hissed as he licked his way down beneath her belly button. "Please."

He obliged, lightly flicking his tongue over her clitoris. Back and forth. Time after time. Until Iris stiffened and cried out, reaching her own strong climax.

"Now, aren't you glad you agreed to have supper with me tonight?" Longarm said.

"Yes, but you haven't fed me, you cheap son of a bitch," she said, laughing.

"Are you hungry?" he asked.

"Of course I'm hungry. Do you know what time it is? We've been lying here screwing for almost two hours," Iris said.

"Huh," Longarm grunted. "Only a woman would keep track o' such things as that."

"Only a *hungry* woman," she corrected.

"Does this mean we gotta get dressed?" he grumbled.

"Only if you don't want to go out on the street naked and get arrested for, well, for whatever they call that sort of thing."

"Indecent exposure," he offered, then sighed. "Fact is, I don't mind getting dressed myself, but I sure as hell hate the idea o' you covering up that pretty body o' yours. Fact is, I like lookin' at you naked."

"Custis, you are a man, and men like to look at any woman naked."

"Yeah, but you're handsomer than most," he said, sitting up and looking around to see where he had tossed his clothes when he and the pretty lady were preparing to do battle. He spotted his balbriggans and reached for them. "It is kinda late, isn't it? I hope we can still be served."

"This is a railroad town," Iris said. "Something is always open."

He grinned and squeezed her left tit. "Something, maybe, but I got something better than mere something in mind, lady."

"Like what, for instance?" she asked.

"Like that fancy place where we ate before. You liked it there, didn't you?"

"Can you afford it again?"

"That wasn't the question I asked you," he said.

"Yes, I liked it," Iris said. "A lot."

"Then let's us go see if they're still serving."

Iris practically leaped out of bed and began hurriedly throwing clothes on, first one outfit and then another, until she arrived at a combination that she thought would be acceptable.

They were only halfway to the hotel when they ran into George Stepanek.

Chapter 28

"You son of a bitch, you haven't paid Mr. Collins your rent yet," Stepanek growled, stepping so close that Longarm could smell the whiskey he had been drinking.

"That's right. I don't owe Mr. Collins anything yet," Longarm said. "And mind your language around the lady. We've discussed this before, you an' me."

"Like hell you don't owe him. It's been almost a month. And I'll talk any way I like since this bitch is no lady."

"George, am I gonna have to beat your ass again?"

"Give me Mr. Collins's money, you cocksucker," Stepanek said.

"First off, our agreement was that he gets a percentage of my profits. I don't have any profit yet. Won't until everything is paid for. So I don't owe the man anything. And I'm telling you clear enough to watch your language around the lady or I will personally teach you some manners, Georgie." Longarm smiled. "Keep in mind that you don't have your bullyboys with you tonight. You don't have anyone to sneak up behind me this time."

Stepanek's answer was to go for the ivory-handled revolver under his left arm.

He was too close for that to be a good idea.

Longarm snatched the gun out of its leather before Stepanek's hand got there. He tossed it into the street, where it bounced into one of the many ruts.

Stepanek tried to return the favor by grabbing at Longarm's holstered .45. That was not any better an idea than going for his own gun had been.

Longarm chopped the edge of his hand down hard on Stepanek's wrist and followed the chop with a punch to Stepanek's gut. He swayed back to give himself a little more room and planted a right cross on Stepanek's jaw. He heard something break. Perhaps the jaw itself or, possibly, probably, just a tooth or two.

George Stepanek cried out aloud and staggered backward. Longarm followed, slinging punches left and right into Stepanek's face until the man reached the edge of the sidewalk boards and tried to step back, only to encounter thin air.

The tall man toppled over backward and landed on his ass in the mouth of an alley.

Longarm glanced at Iris. She was trying—with limited success—to stifle laughter at the sight of Ira Collins's feared enforcer manhandled like that.

Longarm turned to her, bowed and lifted his Stetson in the lady's direction. "My apologies, ma'am. Shall we proceed? I see lights in the dining room there, so we may be in time for the dinner I promised."

Iris took his arm, and he escorted her down the block to the Chauncey Hotel.

They were still serving, and both meal and service were every bit as good as he remembered.

Chapter 29

Longarm had not thought to rent a post office box. Perhaps he should have. It would have made things much more convenient for the local shakedown artists. Instead they—represented presumably by one of Ira Collins's henchmen—left an envelope with his name on it at the front desk of the Pickering Hotel.

"Message for you, Mr. Long," the pimple-faced kid on the desk called when he came in a week or so after his dinner with Iris.

"Thanks, Jersey." For some reason the young fellow loved it when someone referred to him as the Jersey Kid. Longarm supposed the nickname made the youngster feel adventuresome. It did *not* make anyone else think the boy was dangerous.

He carried the message upstairs to read in private. After making sure the room door was locked, he lighted his lamp and turned the wick up high. Then he examined the thing as best he could.

It was the same sort of cheap envelope that Helen had showed him, one of those that had contained threats to her girls.

The message inside was much the same as well. Not threatening to expose Longarm to anyone. He had no one to be exposed to other than Billy Vail, and as far as Billy was concerned Longarm was taking some time off. Lord knew he had accumulated enough vacation time. Unused convalescent time too.

Besides, no one here other than Helen knew that he was a lawman.

YOU ARE IN THE WRONG PLACE. YOU REALLY NEED TO CLOSE UP AND GET OUT BEFORE SOMETHING BAD HAPPENS. THIS IS SENT AS A FRIENDLY WARNING. SO TAKE HEED OR YOU WILL BE HURT.

There was, of course, no signature, nor were there any markings on the envelope to suggest who might have sent it.

Longarm went back downstairs and asked the Jersey Kid who had left the message.

"I don't know, Mr. Long. I took my supper break around six. When I came back on duty, it was there in your slot along with your key. I never saw the person that left it for you. Is that all right? I mean, I didn't do anything wrong, did I?"

Yeah, this was one wild and woolly hombre, all right. Danger on the hoof. "You did exactly right, Jersey. You didn't do anything wrong."

"Thanks, Mr. Long." The boy's smile was wide at discovering he had done nothing wrong and was not in trouble. You would have thought he had just been given a brand-new double eagle.

"Let me know if I get any more messages, Jersey."

"I will, Mr. Long. You can count on me, sir."

"I know I can, Jersey." Longarm smiled at the kid and added, "Hell, I do count on you. Good night, Jersey."

"Good night, sir."

Longarm trudged back upstairs, wondering just what this was all about.

When he thought about it, though, the message was something he could take as a good sign. It meant that Helen's tormentors were starting to expose themselves.

If they wanted to come after him now . . . good! He would love for them to come right out in the open.

He set the latch on his door, but this evening took the extra precaution of propping his room chair under the doorknob. Not that he was expecting company, but a boy never knew about these things.

Chapter 30

Longarm stripped the cheesecloth off a three-pound wedge of cheddar and set it, along with a basket of hardtack, on the end of the counter. There were no customers in the Star at the moment, but soon the lunchtime drinkers would be coming in, and they would want some free eats to go with their beer.

He picked up a cloth and began polishing the bar. Needlessly, as Robert kept things tidy and clean, but at the moment Robert was off getting his own early lunch. He would be back in time to take over for the noon crowd. Or so Longarm hoped. He was not at all sure he could keep up with things by himself.

A bartender's work was more difficult than he had ever realized until he started doing it. Thank goodness for Robert Ware!

The batwings swung open, and a man in a dark suit and wide-brimmed black hat came in.

Longarm fashioned an automatic smile and said, "Welcome. What can I get you?"

By way of an answer the gentleman pulled his coat open

to expose a tin star pinned to his vest. The star and a pistol carried in a shoulder holster.

"I didn't know the town had a marshal," Longarm said.

"It doesn't. I'm Bert Anderson. I'm sheriff of Quapah County. And as such you are in my jurisdiction, Long."

Longarm wiped his hand with a bar rag, then extended it to the sheriff to shake. "Pleased to meet you, Sheriff. Can I offer you a beer or something? Shot of whiskey maybe?"

"I'll take a beer and a shot," Anderson said. "And you and me need to talk."

Longarm poured the shot, leaving the bottle on the bar where Anderson could reach it, then drew the beer chaser and set it in front of the sheriff. "What do we need to talk about, Sheriff?"

Anderson looked around, as if to verify there was no one else in the place to overhear. Then he tossed back the whiskey and took a swallow of beer before he said, "You run some whores in here of an evening."

Longarm nodded. "That's right, Sheriff. I have four girls."

"You aren't licensed to have women. Just the, um, liquid goods."

Longarm could not remember getting a license to run the saloon, never mind the whores. But he was not going to mention that to the county sheriff. "Where do I go to get a license for them?" he asked.

"There is no such license for a saloon," Anderson said. The man poured himself another shot, downed it, and finished the rest of his beer.

"Another?" Longarm asked.

Anderson wiped his mouth with the back of his hand and shook his head. "No, that's enough."

"About that license . . ."

"I told you, there is no such. You aren't allowed to run

whores out of a saloon. Period. Man wants a fuck, he knows where to get it. And it isn't in this saloon or any other around here."

"What am I supposed to do with the girls I already have?" Longarm asked.

"Send them back where they came from. Or sell them. I, um, know a man who would buy them from you. He'd pay you a good price for them. What did you pay for them to begin with?"

"I'd have to look it up," Longarm said. "I disremember at the moment." The truth was that he had gotten the girls from Helen. But he was not going to tell Anderson that. He suspected the sheriff was acting on behalf of Ira Collins more than Quapah County.

"You're being cagey," Anderson said. "That's fine. You don't have to tell me. But you do have to get rid of them. I'll give you to the end of the week. And I'll mention to this man I told you about that you might have some girls you want to sell."

"What if I don't want to sell, Sheriff? What if I get stubborn and keep the girls anyway?"

Anderson shrugged. "Then pretty soon you wouldn't be able to find a supplier for your wet goods. Shipments to you might get lost in transit. You might have trouble hiring help to work your place. And your girls might be . . . shall we say . . . incapacitated." The man gave Longarm a phony smile. "But it's all up to you, Long. You do whatever you think best. I'm just trying to let you know the way things are here. Consider it a favor."

A favor, yes, Longarm thought. But for whom? For Collins more than likely. Certainly it did him no favor.

"I understand, Sheriff. I wouldn't want to do anything out of line here, me not knowin' how things are."

Anderson nodded. "That's the right attitude, Long. Keep that up and you and me will have no problems. Cross me, though, and you could find yourself behind bars."

"Thanks for setting me straight, Sheriff. Are you sure you won't have another before you go?"

"No, thanks. I've had plenty." But the look he gave to the bottle on the bar said that he wanted it. Wanted it bad. The good sheriff, Longarm suspected, was a drunk who had pulled himself together for this little visit.

The man touched the brim of his hat, then turned and left in a hurry. Off to find another drink, Longarm thought, and no harm done. He had done his duty for Collins. Now he was entitled to his reward.

Longarm trailed him as far as the batwings and looked outside. Anderson was met at the end of the block by George Stepanek. The two spoke briefly, then walked together into the Red Lantern Saloon.

Longarm went back to his own bar and put the glasses Anderson had used into the washtub, where they would be washed and dried before being returned to the shelves later.

He hoped Robert got back before the noon crowd started showing up.

Chapter 31

Longarm dropped the satchel containing the day's receipts onto the floor beside Helen's desk. He was using her safe to hold the earnings of the Star since he did not have a safe of his own. Buying one had seemed an unnecessary extravagance since he did not intend to be in business very long, just until he smoked out Helen's problems for her.

He slumped gratefully into an upholstered chair and accepted the glass of rye she poured for him.

"Thanks," he said, taking a swallow of the excellent whiskey. He set the glass aside—being around liquor all day was beginning to take the edge off his enjoyment of it; very much more and he would be in danger of becoming a teetotaler—and reached for a cheroot.

Helen waited until he had the cigar lighted, then said, "So how did it go with our esteemed sheriff today?"

Longarm raised an eyebrow. "Jeez, woman, do you know everything that happens around here?"

Helen laughed. "If I did, Custis, I wouldn't have asked you for help. Actually, this morning was the time when the working girls in town are allowed to shop. They saw Anderson going into your place. Three of them told me about it. They thought something was up. Two of them suggested you might be secretly working for the other side."

"They know what's going on," Longarm said.

"Not really. I already told you, most of them are dumb as fence posts. But they can be sly, and most of them understand lies and betrayal well enough. God knows they've experienced enough of both before they ever come to my houses. I'm careful to *not* give them any more of the same here, which is why they learn to trust me and why some would want to tip me off if they saw or heard anything that could hurt me."

"You live an interesting life, Helen. It must be eye-opening in a lot o' ways," he said.

"More than I ever expected when I, um, entered the business," Helen said.

Longarm chuckled at the thought of how disconcerting it must have been for a prim and proper bookkeeper, which Helen had been at the time, to inherit a whorehouse.

"So go on, Custis. Tell me about the sheriff and what he wanted with you," Helen said.

Longarm polished off the glass of rye and looked Helen in the eye. He sighed and said, "Trouble."

Chapter 32

"So they're starting with you now," Helen mused, "and they are using the sheriff. I wonder if that miserable son of a bitch even knows who he's working for. And why."

"He can be bought?" Longarm asked.

Helen grunted her disdain for the Quapah County sheriff. "Like a can of beans," she said. "Probably about as cheap too."

"Have you tried to buy him?" Longarm asked.

"Oh, I do. I pay him off the first day of each and every month. Ten dollars for each girl."

"So he works for Collins," Longarm said.

"You would think so, but to tell you the truth I'm not sure about that. I've heard rumors that suggest there may be someone else pulling the strings behind Anderson."

Longarm rose and helped himself to a small refresher on his drink, then leaned down and kissed the large woman lightly on the forehead. "We'll figure it out," he assured her.

"I hope so. My girls got some more of those letters. More of the same. Do you want to see them?"

"They're the same bullshit as before?" he asked.

Helen nodded. "The same. Same envelopes, same penciled handwriting, same old crap."

"No need for me to look at them then, not when I have one of my own to admire."

"Is there any way to trace mail back to its origin?" Helen asked.

"Not that I know about, but I think it's about time that I talk with the postmaster here. Maybe he knows something that would help."

"She," Helen said.

"Pardon?"

"I said 'she.' Our postmaster is really a postmistress. We have a woman in the job. Her late husband was a big supporter of the governor. Big contributor too, I gather. When he died, the widow discovered that the rat had been living well beyond their means. She was broke. Either she told the governor or someone else did, because he found out about it and secured an appointment for her as postmistress. Now she lives on what she earns in that capacity."

"Unusual," Longarm said, taking first a drag on his cheroot and then a swallow of Helen's good rye. He wished he could keep a bottle of whiskey that good in the Star, but if he did, someone was bound to pour from it for a bar patron, and in his opinion that would be a hell of a waste. Set a bad precedent too, because soon everyone would want the good stuff, and any chance of making a profit would go out the window.

"Do you need any more money to run your joint?" Helen asked.

Longarm aimed his cheroot toward the satchel he had set on the floor earlier. "There's your answer. I don't know that we're making a profit yet. Probably not. But we're bringing in money. Won't be long until the setup costs are met and you should be pulling in a profit."

Helen laughed. "Not me. You're the proprietor there."

"We both know better, darlin'. I'll be gone before long an' you'll have the place all to yourself."

"Will I be able to trust Robert to run the place for me when that happens, Custis?"

"Absolutely. Robert is a good man. I trust him."

"Do you think he is talking with Collins behind your back?"

"If I did," Longarm said, "I wouldn't be recommending him to you."

"Something else I just thought about, Custis. Are you remembering to pay yourself a salary for running the place?"

He shook his head. "I draw my pay from Uncle Sam. That's enough for me." He laughed. "But I'm not above treating myself to a glass of bar whiskey or a pocketful of smokes now and then."

"You help yourself to anything you want, dear. I'm just grateful you are taking the time to help me."

"Not that I've been much help so far," he said.

"You're here. That is enough to make this old woman happy. Is there anything I can get you, dear? Anything I can do for you?"

Chapter 33

In the morning Longarm made sure things at the Star were running smoothly—or as smoothly as things seemed to get in a railroad town saloon—then turned it over to Robert.

"I have some errands to run," he said, wiping his hands with a bar rag. "No idea how long I'll be. Not long, I think."

"Take your time," Ware told him. "I can handle things until you get back."

"I know you can," Longarm said with a smile. "Thanks."

He removed the apron he had taken to wearing when he was behind the bar and retrieved his tweed coat from a hook he had screwed into the wall.

"I won't be long."

He walked to the post office, a block and a half away from the Pickering Hotel. The clerk behind the counter was a man, a stocky fellow with dark hair and a hairline mustache on his upper lip.

"Yes, sir, how can I help you?" The man had a rugged enough appearance, but his voice was soft, almost feminine. Longarm had seen him in the Star a few times, always in the company of a skinny man, always more interested in playing cards than drinking.

"I'd like to see the postmistress."

"If you have a complaint, sir, I'm sure I can take care of it for you."

"What I would like is to see the postmistress," Longarm repeated.

"Very well, sir. Just a moment." The clerk left the counter and disappeared into a back room. He returned after less than a minute and pointed toward the bank of postal boxes. "Back there, sir. She will meet you at the door."

Longarm hadn't noticed that there was a door beyond the lockboxes, but it was obvious enough when he looked for it.

Postmistress Anne Gilbert emerged after several minutes. She was tall, slim, and elegant. She had hair so pale he was not sure if it was blond or gray. Her age might have been anything from thirty to fifty. He simply could not tell. She wore her hair pinned up in a tight bun and had a black velvet choker at her throat, with a cameo brooch. Longarm started to feel the stirrings of a hard-on when he saw her.

"Yes, sir?"

It took him a moment to answer. He would have preferred to just stand and stare at her for a few minutes. Anne Gilbert was far and away the best-looking woman he had seen in some time.

"Yes, sir?" she repeated. "Barney said someone was out here wanting to see me. Would that be you, sir?"

Longarm cleared his throat and reminded himself to pay attention to business. "Yes, ma'am. And I assume you're Mrs. Gilbert?"

The lady nodded. "I am. How may I help you?"

"Is there some place private where we could talk?" he asked.

"We could go in the back. I have a desk there," she said.

He nodded and followed her inside. There was the usual sorting table, a bin of outgoing mail, and several empty mailbags. The postmaster's desk was stuck away in a corner.

"Now. This is as private as we get, so what do you want to tell me?"

Longarm smiled. "Now that I think about it, this ain't really private enough. Maybe we could talk over dinner tonight instead." The smile turned into a grin. "My treat at the Chauncey." The place was devilishly expensive, but what the hell, Helen was paying for it.

Anne Gilbert said nothing, and for a moment he thought he had offended her. Then she relaxed. "We close at six."

"I'll come by for you then," he said, touching the brim of his Stetson and nodding to the lady. "Six o'clock. Sharp."

Longarm turned and left.

Chapter 34

The noontime rush went off well enough. The Star seemed to be gaining something of a reputation, as men from all the various business factions—railroaders, miners, cowboys, and townspeople alike—were choosing it to do their drinking.

It took both Longarm and Robert Ware working pretty much full-time to keep up with the demand. The customers came in steadily, but no one took on more booze than he could handle.

"I'd count this something of a success," Longarm said.

"Treat people right," Ware winked and chuckled, "and beat the competition's prices, and you can count on it being a success. Mind if I mention something, Boss?"

"Of course not. Say anything you like, Robert," Longarm said.

"Forgive me for saying so, but I don't think you have a lot of experience with running a saloon."

"It shows, huh?" Longarm said with a rueful smile.

Ware nodded. "It shows. For instance, you need to reorder your beer and your bar whiskey. Thanks to the railroad it will only take two, maybe three days for the goods to get here, but the thing is, you don't want to run out. If the patrons think they can't count on getting what they want here, they will go somewhere else. This is not the only saloon in town. They have others they could go to, some of them closer to the railroad depot and easier to get to. You need to put your orders in now while you have plenty of time before we'll run out of anything."

"I hadn't thought o' that," Longarm admitted.

"And that is why I get the idea you're a mite new to this business," Ware said.

"I'm glad I found you," Longarm said. "You know the business, and the customers seem to like you. You have enough experience that I'm a little surprised you don't have a place of your own."

"I don't have the kind of capital it takes to open my own place or I would," Ware said. "But I do have experience. I've run saloons for other owners." He hesitated, then took a deep breath. "I like you, Mr. Long. There is something I should tell you."

"Anything, Robert. You can tell me anything," Longarm said.

"When I first walked in to apply for the job . . . I was sent here."

"Oh? By who?"

Again Ware hesitated. "I was sent here by Mr. Collins. He knew I was looking for a job after I quit Wash Howard at the Deuces. Son of a bitch tried to cheat me. But that's neither here nor there. Mr. Collins suggested I come here. For a couple reasons, I think. One is the obvious. He wants you to do well because he is in for a share of your profits. Don't look at me like that, Mr. Long. It's no great secret the way Mr. Collins works. The other reason, I think, is so I can keep an eye on you. He likes you, but I'm not sure he trusts you."

"Has he asked you to report anything back to him?" Longarm asked.

"Not directly, but the bookkeeper is his man. I'm sure he tells Mr. Collins everything he knows. And he asks me questions sometimes that I think go right back to Mr. Collins."

"That's interesting," Longarm said. "But there is nothing about the Star that I wouldn't want Collins to know, so don't you worry about being disloyal. You do whatever is comfortable for you an' don't worry about it none. I won't mind. I'd appreciate it if you'd tell me what you pass along to Collins, but you don't have to. Just keep on doing what you have been, an' you and me will get along just fine."

Longarm paused to fetch a cheroot for himself out of the humidor and to offer one to Ware; then he said, "If you don't mind I'm gonna go have my lunch now. The crowd has thinned out enough that I reckon you can handle it by yourself."

"Take your time, Mr. Long," Ware said.

Longarm smiled. "That's Custis to you, Robert."

"In that case, sir, if you don't mind, I really prefer Bob with my friends. Robert is for business."

"Bob it is then."

"Enjoy your lunch, Custis."

Chapter 35

Tisbury's was empty of customers when Longarm got there. Apparently the always busy lunch crowd had had their meals and gone back to the afternoon's work.

Longarm took a seat in a corner, by habit placing his back to something solid. He ordered steak, well done and smothered in milk gravy, plus biscuits with more of that gravy, and asked, "Would it be possible for a man t' get a mess o' eggs at this hour of the day?"

Tisbury grunted. "How many do you want?"

"Four if you have them to spare."

"I can cook you all you like up to and including six dozen." He smiled. "But four eggs it will be."

Longarm worked on a cup of stout coffee while Tisbury went back to his stove to make Longarm's steak and eggs. He was halfway through the coffee when someone he thought was one of the men who'd jumped him in the street several weeks past came in.

The man, shaggy and unshaven, hung his hat on a rack beside the door and said to Tisbury, "It looks like it's coming rain." His remark was punctuated by the sound of thunder outside.

He took a seat on one of the stools at the counter and asked for coffee, then swiveled his stool around. The man glanced idly in Longarm's direction. His casual demeanor changed like a flash of the lightning that flickered beyond the windows.

Recognizing that he was not alone in the café, he saw who the other customer was. He instantly stiffened, his whole body going rigid. His right hand formed into a claw that hovered over the gutta-percha grips of the revolver on his hip.

Aside from the possibility of him being one of his attackers, Longarm did not think he had ever seen the man before. Certainly he was not a patron of the Star saloon.

But the fellow recognized Longarm. And seemed to fear him.

His hand leaped toward that revolver.

Longarm had no idea why.

But he did not have time to ponder the question or to ask why. The man was drawing on him. That was introduction enough.

Longarm's .45 came to hand almost without him taking time to consciously reach for it.

His Colt spat its own brand of thunder and lightning as flame and smoke—and lead—belched from the muzzle.

Across the width of the café floor Longarm's first bullet took the man in the belly.

A second struck him high in the chest. And a third ripped into the left side of his face.

"Jesus!" Tisbury screamed.

Longarm came to his feet and stood poised to fire again if necessary. A fourth bullet was not needed. The man, a complete stranger as far as Longarm knew for sure, crumpled. He toppled face-forward onto Tisbury's floor. He fell like a sack of grain, making no move to soften the blow or prepare for it. Once he hit, he lay completely motionless.

Longarm coughed as smoke from the black powder cartridges filled the café. His ears rang a little from the contained concussion, and the sounds were hollow and dull when Tisbury said, "Jesus, Long. What . . . ?"

"Damned if I know. I'm not sure I ever saw the son of a bitch before, but he sure as hell recognized me. You saw him go for his gun, didn't you?"

Tisbury said nothing, so Longarm said again, "You saw him reach, didn't you? Well, didn't you?"

Tisbury remained silent.

"What the hell are you doing, man? You saw. You saw I didn't have a choice," Longarm barked. He crossed the room to stand nose to nose with Tisbury and said it again. "You saw that he drew on me. You saw I had no choice." His words came not as a question but as a statement of fact. "What are you worried about anyway, Tisbury? This town don't have no regular law, and Sheriff Anderson damn sure isn't around. Not that I'd expect him to do anything if he was. This was simple self-defense, no less."

Still the café owner stood mute. After a moment he turned and fetched a mop and bucket. Silently the man began to clean up the blood that had spilled onto his floor.

Longarm stood for a moment staring down at the mop swishing back and forth beside the corpse. Then he turned and left Tisbury's. It was obvious he was not going to get his meal. He had no idea who would collect the body and haul it off to . . . he had no idea where. An undertaker's, perhaps. Or simply to an ice house where the thing could be kept from rotting until someone came to claim it.

Longarm did not even know for sure who the man was. He thought the fellow might have been one of the three who jumped him—also without provocation—that night a little while back.

Whoever he was, Tisbury seemed to be in fear for some reason about his death. But in fear of what, or of whom, Longarm did not know.

What he did know was that he was still hungry.

He went in search of a different café where he could get something to eat.

Chapter 36

"Are you Mr. Long?" The youngster asking the question was likely in his teens, with the bright red pimples and peach fuzzed upper lip to announce the fact.

Longarm looked up from his steak—but no eggs in this café—and nodded.

"Mr. Collins wants to see you," the boy said.

"All right. Thanks." Longarm went back to sawing at the tough slab of meat with a table knife that was much too dull for the task. The messenger boy remained standing beside his table.

Longarm grunted and reached into his pocket, found a nickel for a tip, and handed it over. Still the boy stood there.

"Is there something else?"

"It's just . . . when Mr. Collins wants to see somebody, they most generally go," the boy said. "Right away."

"Well I ain't 'somebody,' and there's nothing I got to say to Mr. Collins. If he wants to see me, I ain't hard to find. You managed just fine."

"Sir, I can't . . . I can't say something like that to Mr. Collins," the kid stammered out, backing away a half step as if he expected Longarm to reach out and hit him.

Longarm merely shrugged. And took another bite of the exceptionally tough chunk of beef. Damn, but he wished he had gotten that meal at Tisbury's. At least the steak there was reasonably tender. And Tisbury made a better gravy than these people too.

The messenger boy turned and left. Finally. Longarm looked up from his meal for a moment to watch the boy out the door.

Then he went back to his delayed lunch.

Chapter 37

"Anything happen while I was at lunch, Bob?" Longarm asked when he returned to the Star Saloon. His saloon. His very own. He was still having a little difficulty accepting that reality.

"No, Boss, but I hear there was plenty happening around you," Ware answered.

"Word does seem to travel fast around here," Longarm said.

"Believe it," Ware told him.

There were two mid-afternoon drinkers propping up the bar with their elbows. When they saw Longarm come in, they shifted down to the other end of the bar, separating themselves from him and from any trouble he might bring with him.

Three men playing cards at one of the tables eyed him carefully, but they remained where they were.

Longarm was beginning to feel like something of a celebrity here. Or a pariah. He walked behind the bar and drew a beer for himself. Then he took a deck of cards from a shelf and went out to one of the tables to begin playing solitaire.

If the sheriff—or anyone else—wanted him, dammit, he did not intend to be hard to find.

The two buzzards at the bar tossed back the rest of their drinks and skedaddled. The three playing cards threw their hands in, scooped up their coins, and hurried out. Even Bob Ware grabbed a towel and drifted to the far end of the bar, just as far from the door as he could get.

Standing near the doors onto the street was Ira Collins.

Longarm leaned back in his chair and waited for the man to do whatever it was he came here for.

Collins did not appear to be carrying a gun. Of course he could have had half a dozen well-concealed hide-out guns, and no one would likely know.

The little man, or big man depending on how one wanted to look at him, glanced around the room but patiently waited until the customers cleared out before he approached the table where Longarm was sitting.

"Mind if I join you?" he asked.

"Help yourself," Longarm said, one boot pushing a chair out.

Collins sat down.

"Can I offer you something to drink? We have whiskey or beer, your choice. Or both."

"Nothing for me, thanks. I won't be here but a moment, Long. There is something I want to make clear to you," the town boss said.

"All right. Say your piece."

"It's about Kenny."

Longarm raised an eyebrow. "Kenny? Who would that be?"

"Kenneth Milbank. He is the man you shot at Tisbury's."

"I never knew his name," Longarm said.

"Kenny worked for me. You may have heard that."

"Nope. Kinda thought so, but I didn't know it for sure," Longarm said.

"Yes, well, he did. But I want you to know, Long, that I had no part in that assassination attempt on your life. Kenny was not acting on my behalf when he tried to kill you."

"You know that he drew first, I take it," Longarm said.

Collins nodded. "I already spoke with Tisbury about it. He admitted to me that he saw the whole thing. Kenny walked into the café, sat down, and when he saw you he tried to kill you. It is as plain as that."

"Interesting," Longarm said. "When I asked him if he'd seen it, he didn't say aye or nay, just stood there with his mouth shut."

"He was, shall we say, worried that he might say the wrong thing. All I asked him for was the truth," Collins said. "He told me what happened, and there will be no charges filed against you."

"The man did work for you, though," Longarm said.

Collins nodded. "He did."

"An' he was one of them that mugged me an' stole my money a while back."

"I believe he was, yes," Collins admitted.

"But you had nothin' to do with this time."

"That's right. Kenny was not acting under my orders. I want you to know that." Collins fashioned a small smile. "After all, I am expecting to gain some profit from your business here. It would make no sense for me to have you killed. Think of all the profits I would lose. I am a businessman, after all. It is your profit that I want, not your life."

"Makes sense," Longarm conceded. "But what about the mugging?"

"That was a misunderstanding. It was discussed. And corrected," Collins said. "I doubt it will need to be repeated."

The smile broadened. “You are a businessman too. I am sure you understand these things.”

Longarm was tempted to ask, that being so, why Collins was set on ruining Helen, but he bit back the notion. He did not believe Ira Collins knew about his connection with Helen. He certainly did not believe Collins knew he was a deputy United States marshal, and it was probably best that that remain so.

“Thanks for tellin’ me the shooting was his own idea,” Longarm said. “Naturally it crossed my mind that you might’ve wanted it done.”

“Trust me about this, Long. If I had wanted you dead, I would have sent more than one man. And you would be dead now.”

Collins stood, touched the brim of his narrow-brimmed hat, and left.

Only when he was gone did customers begin to return to the Star.

Chapter 38

"Bob? When you get a minute?" Longarm gestured to his second-in-command, then picked up the cards and resumed his game of solitaire.

Three or four minutes later, Robert Ware made sure everyone at the bar was taken care of then came over to the table where Longarm was seated.

"Sit down, Bob," Longarm said.

Ware chose a seat where he could keep an eye on the bar and hustle over there if anyone wanted a refill. "Yeah, Boss?"

"I had me an interesting talk with Collins." Longarm outlined the gist of the conversation then asked, "What d'you think about it, Bob?"

Ware thought for a moment, then said, "He could be telling the truth. Especially when he said if he wanted you dead he would've sent the whole bunch of Stepanek's people, not just the one man."

"Maybe, but that one . . . Kenny something, Collins said he was . . . That man didn't come into Tisbury's looking for a gunfight. He sat at the counter and ordered something. It was only when he noticed me in that back corner that he got his hackles up an' went for his gun. It was happenstance, not planned."

"It sounds personal to me," Ware said. "Just a minute. That fella at the end of the bar needs a refill. I'll be right back." Ware left the table and hurried back behind the bar to attend to the customer.

Longarm watched him, but his concentration was on Ira Collins, not Robert Ware.

When he returned to the table, Ware asked, "Is there anything else, Boss?"

"Just wonderin' what your thoughts are," Longarm said.

"To be honest, Custis, it's possible Collins was lying. Not about Kenneth but about wanting you to make a go of it here. I happen to think that if you were to be killed before you start paying Collins for the rent on this place, he could foreclose on the Star and take it over. That would give him a hundred percent of the profit on something you've developed. You did the work. He would reap the profit."

"He wouldn't run the place himself," Longarm said.

"He would probably hire me to run it for him," Ware said. "I already know the trade, the customers, the ordering procedures. And Collins thinks I'm working for him anyway."

"Is he paying you?" Longarm asked.

Ware grinned. "No, Boss, he's letting you do that for him."

"Interesting," Longarm said.

"Excuse me. I'd best get back behind the bar. Those fellows over there are just about to the bottom of their glasses. They'll be wanting refills soon."

Longarm nodded, and Robert Ware went back to work.

Longarm wanted to talk with Helen about this, especially about the point Bob Ware had raised that Collins could foreclose if anything happened to Longarm. It probably would be a good idea for him to get something in writing with Helen. As an investor, perhaps, or showing that she had loaned him the funds to get started. That way she could claim the Star if Longarm were gunned down.

He would have gone to her as soon as it got dark, but he had promised to take Anne Gilbert to dinner at the Chauncey.

Later, then, would have to do.

Ira Collins had certainly *seemed* genuine when he spoke.

Longarm just wished that he knew where the truth lay with the man.

He picked up the cards again and once more resumed playing. But his thoughts were far from solitaire, allowing his mind to work on his problems unconsciously while he slapped the cards down and moved them from place to place on the table before him.

Chapter 39

Longarm walked down to the railroad depot and sent a telegram to his Denver supplier ordering four more barrels of beer, and while he was in the vicinity, he asked that Cory Dreason be notified to get the carter to pick up the barrels when they arrived and haul them over to the Star.

From there he headed for the Pickering and his room so he could wash up before he met Anne Gilbert for dinner.

"Message for you, Mr. Long."

He changed direction, turning from the staircase and heading for the desk. "Thanks, Jersey," he said when the youngster handed him an envelope that could have been a twin to the one he had gotten before.

"Where'd this come from, Jersey? Who brought it?"

"Andy brought it, Mr. Long."

"And who would Andy be?"

"He's just a kid. Runs errands. Does odd jobs. I see him around," the desk clerk said.

"Does Andy have a last name?"

"Oh, I'm sure he does, but I've never heard what it is."

"Do you know where Andy lives?" Longarm asked.

"No, sir."

"How d'you think I might go about finding him then?"

"You see him hanging around on the street sometimes," Jersey said. "Mostly over by the train station."

"All right, thanks."

Longarm changed his mind about going up to his room and having a wash. Instead he spun on his heels and headed for the railroad depot to see if he could find this Andy.

He stuffed the envelope—unopened—into his pocket. There really seemed no need to read whatever it contained. He felt sure it would just be another warning that he get out.

That was almost a compliment. It meant he was annoying someone. With any luck at all, that someone he was pissing off would be the same person who was trying to ruin Helen's trade by frightening her whores.

Two birds with one stone.

But first he had to smoke the son of a bitch out into the open.

Chapter 40

"Sure, I know who you mean," the stationmaster said. "Andy Warner. I see him here all the time. He's a good kid. Handy to have around. He does odd jobs. Runs errands. Like that."

"Did you see him today?" Longarm asked. "This afternoon?"

The railroad man nodded. "Yes. Saw him here, oh, I'd say it's been an hour or so. But he isn't here now. He went off with a couple fellows."

"For a job?"

"I wouldn't know where they were going or what they wanted with Andy," the stationmaster said.

Longarm pulled out a cheroot, hesitated, then offered it to the stationmaster and got out another for himself. He bit the twist off the end of his cigar, struck a match, and lighted both before he asked, "Do you know who these fellas were?"

The railroader shook his head. "Don't know their names or anything like that, but I've seen them around town. They don't hang around down here, though. You mostly see them with George Stepanek. Do you know him?"

"Oh, I know George, all right. These men that Andy went with. You say they're friends of Stepanek?"

"I don't know if they're friends or what, but you see them together a lot. Them and there's a third one. But I heard he got killed, so I guess it's just two of them now to do Stepanek's dirty work."

"What do you mean when you say 'dirty work'?" Longarm asked.

The stationmaster blinked. "I . . . I said too much." He looked down at the cheroot in his hand as if accusing it of making him say more than he should. For a moment Longarm thought he was going to throw the cigar on the ground to rid himself of the offending article.

The man suddenly clammed up. He spun around and practically fled back into the depot without a word of apology.

Longarm grunted his own displeasure. Wherever Stepanek's cronies had taken Andy Warner, it was clear that Longarm was not going to speak with him. Not now at any rate.

He pulled out his bulbous Ingersoll and checked the time. Anne Gilbert had said she would be through work at six. He barely had enough time to wash up, change his shirt, and get back to the post office to pick her up for their dinner date.

He would have to leave off looking for Warner until tomorrow.

He turned and headed at a fast walk back to the Pickering.

Chapter 41

Longarm exited the Chauncey, Anne Gilbert on his arm and a pleasantly warm sensation in his belly, put there by a truly excellent dinner.

"I can't tell you how long it has been since I had such a nice time," the postmistress said. "Thank you, Custis."

"Believe me, it was my pleasure. You're good company. Nice to be around."

"Thank you." She gave his elbow a slight squeeze to emphasize the comment.

"You're gonna have to lead the way to your place," Longarm said. "I don't know where you live."

"You don't have to walk me home," the lady said. "I'm perfectly safe by myself."

"I wouldn't think of letting you go off alone," he told her.

"Very well then." She smiled. "It isn't far."

Seven or eight minutes later, Anne stopped in front of a modest bungalow with a wide front porch and flower beds flanking the walkway. "My hobby," she explained. The lady hesitated, seeming indecisive about something. Then she said, "Will you come in for a brandy, Custis?"

He opened the gate and escorted her through the avenue of flowers and onto the porch. Anne opened the door. It was not locked.

"You're a trusting soul," he said.

"Oh, nothing ever happens here," Anne said.

Longarm was not sure he shared that view. In fact, he very much did not. He wondered what it must be like to be so sure of one's fellow citizens the way Anne Gilbert was. It was a confidence he was sure he would never experience.

"Wait here. I'll light a lamp," she said.

Longarm stood in the doorway while she moved away, disappearing into the foyer. After a moment he saw the flare of a match. Anne lifted the globe of a lamp and touched the flame to the wick, then adjusted the wick to a soft flutter and went on to light two more lamps before she returned to him.

"In here," she said, leading the way into a comfortably furnished parlor.

Longarm settled into the armchair that he assumed must once have been her husband's. There was a lamp beside it and a book with a page marker in it, so Anne must favor the comfortable chair now that she was alone in the house.

"You have no children?" he asked.

"No. We tried, but . . . no."

"That's a shame," he said, not sure if he meant it or not. Children would have given her company in the house. But children could be a pain in the ass too.

"Let me get you that brandy," she said.

Brandy was not one of his favorite tipples, but he could handle it when he had to. Anne left him alone in the parlor while she went into a back room, presumably the kitchen, and returned moments later with two snifters of brandy.

While she was back there, she had taken her hair down from the severe bun she'd worn during the day. Her hair was long, platinum white, and hanging in soft curls past her shoulders.

"Do you mind?" she asked.

"It's lovely," he said. Then he smiled and added, "But so are you, Anne. Very lovely."

"Do you really think so?"

"Oh, yes. You're beautiful."

She set the brandies aside and came to him, folding herself into his lap and wrapping her arms around Longarm's neck. "I know I am being terribly brazen, but . . ."

"Shh." He kissed her. A few minutes later he stood, picking Anne up, and asked, "Which way?"

She pointed him toward her bedroom.

Chapter 42

Anne Gilbert was even better looking naked than clothed. And in Longarm's opinion, such a woman was a rare and wonderful thing.

She was tall and slim, with small breasts and small, rather pale nipples that pointed upward. Her waist was tiny, her hips rounded and smooth. Her back was long and lean, as were her legs. She had a nearly flat belly and a softly fluffy bush of blond hair.

Anne's mouth was soft. Tasty too, he discovered, and her tongue was mobile as it probed his own.

"Do you mind?" she asked as she knelt over him, moving from his mouth down to his nipples. She licked him there, then her tongue ranged lower still. Across his belly to his prick.

She took him into her mouth, the warmth engulfing his cock as he strained upward, wanting more of the sensations she was giving him. A thin string of spittle ran from the tip of his dick to Anne's lower lip when she pulled back from him.

She cupped his balls in the palm of her hand and returned

her mouth to his rigid cock. She sucked him for a moment then ran the tip of her tongue down his shaft and onto his balls.

Longarm pulled her to him and buried his own tongue in her soft and fragrant bush. Perfumed, he thought.

His tongue found the wet opening to her pussy. Anne moaned aloud when he began to lick the tiny button of her pleasure. After only seconds she shuddered and writhed, her slender body wracked by the throes of a powerful orgasm.

He returned to what he was doing, but she pushed him away. "Too much," she mumbled, her mouth full of cock. "Strong. So long since . . . It's been a long time since I felt that. Too powerful."

Longarm kissed her inner thighs and ran his hands over her tits, cupping them, gently squeezing.

"Please," she said, pulling away from him. "Fuck me now."

She stretched out on the bed beside him and parted her legs to receive him as Longarm moved on top of her.

Anne stiffened and lifted her hips to ease his entry into her wet and gaping pussy. She was slim; he could feel her hip bones gouge into his lower belly.

Longarm filled her. The heat of Anne's body surrounded him, took his cock deep inside as she held him tight with arms and legs alike.

Again it took only seconds before she shuddered. He could feel the lips of her pussy flutter and clench with the power of her climax.

He did not hold back then, driving hard and deep and seeking his own powerful climax, his cum spewing into her quivering body.

"Thank you. Oh, thank you," Anne whispered into his ear.

Longarm nuzzled the side of her neck and buried his face in that soft, pale hair, his cock still inside Anne's body.

Minutes later he could feel the return of his need. His cock stiffened once more and he began slowly and gently to rock in and out. Anne responded, and he began to think that this might be a long and exceptionally pleasant night ahead.

The Star Saloon could just take care of itself for the evening.

Chapter 43

It was sometime in the small hours of the morning when Longarm slipped out of Anne Gilbert's back door, careful lest her neighbors see that she had had a male visitor in the darkened house. Anne came to the door with him, naked and lovely, and gave him a parting kiss.

"You are quite a man, Custis Long. I hope you are here to stay," she told him.

Longarm refrained from correcting that hope. He missed Denver. He missed his job. But Helen was a friend, and he would not have thought of abandoning her until he eliminated her problem here. The bottom line was that Helen needed him.

Thinking of her after leaving Anne, Longarm suddenly changed direction and headed toward the whorehouse.

From an alley mouth half a block ahead, in the direction he had been walking, a bright fan of flame exploded.

He saw the muzzle flash. Heard the whip of the bullet as it passed close by. Heard the dull, flat report of the gunshot.

Without taking time to consciously think of what he should

do in response, Longarm hunkered low and charged straight toward the unknown assailant, his .45 in hand.

Longarm's Colt roared, belching flame and smoke. And lead.

He heard his bullet strike wood. Close enough to the son of a bitch, he hoped, to chase the bastard away.

Half-blinded by his own muzzle flare, Longarm fired again, with no better result this time. In truth he was not even sure the shooter remained in that alley mouth. Nor whose damn alley it was.

He got there to find nothing and nobody. The alley was a narrow gap between a barbershop—it reminded him that he could use a trim—and a mining implements store.

In the same block were a saddle shop, closed at that hour of course, and a saloon.

A man came wobbling out of the saloon, but when he saw Longarm he smiled and touched the brim of his hat and went staggering on.

There was no sign of the person who had shot at him.

Longarm slid his Colt back into leather and resumed his walk toward Helen Morrow's fanciest whorehouse.

After being with Anne Gilbert he had no need to get laid, but he certainly did want to talk with Helen.

Chapter 44

"You certainly have Ira Collins stirred up if he is going so far as to have you murdered," Helen said, offering solace in the form of her first-rate rye whiskey.

"The son of a bitch can try," Longarm said. "But trying ain't the same as doing."

Longarm downed the first double shot and held his glass out for a refill. That one he drank more slowly, enjoying the flavor and the bite on his tongue.

"Has to be Collins," Longarm said. "But the man sounded sincere when I spoke with him. He said he wouldn't want to lose the profit he expects to make out of the Star. I believed him then. Now . . ."

"Don't trust that man, Custis. Not for a minute. He's a snake. Worse than a snake. At least a snake rattles before it strikes." She sat down ponderously, the flaps of loose skin under her arms swaying. "I don't suppose you saw who shot at you," Helen said.

"Of course not. It was dark . . . What the hell time is it

anyway? I'm fairly sure I didn't hit anything but the side of a building when I fired back at him."

Helen opened what he thought was a large brooch pinned to the bosom of her gown. It turned out to be a watch instead. "It is three-forty-seven," she said.

Longarm smiled. "Time for good little children to be asleep in their beds," he said.

"That leaves you out, Custis. You are neither good nor little. What have you been up to at this hour? It's obvious you have not been out carousing, not even at the Star."

He shook his head and took another sip of the whiskey. "Never you mind where I been an' what I been up to." He grinned over the rim of his glass, set the rye aside, and reached for a cheroot.

"I wish I could do more for you, Custis, but I've had my girls . . . the ones I can trust, anyway . . . listening for anything that might help."

"How is your business, Helen?" he asked.

"Wonderful as far as that goes. I get plenty of business. If Collins will leave my girls alone, I'll have a gold mine here."

"Are the real mines digging gold?"

"No, they aren't bringing gold out of the ground. They're mining coal. But it is all golden to me when the boys come spend their pay with my girls," she said.

"We'll figure this out," Longarm said, not sure if he believed it or not. He finished his whiskey and set the glass aside before he lighted his cheroot. He blew a few smoke rings toward the ceiling of Helen's office. Then he stood.

"Reckon I should get to bed," he said. "This old boy ain't as spry as he used to be."

Helen laughed. "Liar," she said accusingly. "We should all be in as good a shape as you are."

"Spry enough, maybe, but for damn sure sleepy. I'm gonna

head back to the hotel and catch a little sleep." He bent down and kissed her on the cheek. "G'night, sweetie."

"Good night, Custis." Helen frowned. "Be careful going home. That man tonight . . . you never know when he might try again."

Longarm grinned. "Yeah, but next time it's my turn."

"I hope so. But if you don't mind, I will pray for you, Custis."

"Why, Helen, you're serious, ain't you?" He smiled and touched her cheek. "Don't you worry 'bout me. I have it on good authority that I'm too mean for heaven, an' the devil don't want me neither."

Laughing, he headed out into the night and turned his steps toward the Pickering and a much needed bed—but this time to actually sleep in it.

Chapter 45

"Good morning, Boss," Robert Ware said. "I'm sorry to wake you, but we have a, um, well, a situation over at the saloon."

Longarm stepped back from the hotel room door and tried to rub the sleep out of his eyes. "What the hell, Bob. What time z'it, anyway?"

"Five, five-thirty, something like that," Ware said.

"Come in. Sit down an' tell me what's going on." Longarm went to his washstand and splashed a little water from the pitcher into the washbasin. He dipped both hands into the water and patted it onto his face in an attempt to wake up. It helped.

"The thing is, Boss . . ."

"Custis," Longarm corrected.

"Right. Well, the thing is, Custis, a little while ago Bucky Doyle came and woke me. He said he closed up about three-thirty and went down the street to find some friends to share a nightcap. Likely they went to the Chinaman's for a pipe of opium, but what he said was 'nightcap.' "

"Opium? I didn't know Bucky liked that stuff," Longarm said.

"Yeah, well, it doesn't seem to do him any harm. I mean, he isn't hooked or anything. Anyway that's not why I'm here now."

"Sorry. Go on, Bob."

"Yes, well, just a little while ago Bucky and two of his friends were on their way back to Bucky's place. Bucky noticed that the front door of the Star was ajar. He was sure he had closed and locked it before he left." Ware frowned. "Bucky wouldn't have left the door open, Boss. He just wouldn't."

"All right. Go on."

"They looked inside. The place was busted up, Boss. They busted the spigot out of the beer barrel; there's beer all over the floor 'cause naturally it all ran out, everything that was left in that barrel. A lot of the glasses were busted, so there's broken glass mixed in with the spilled beer.

"Naturally I ran over there and took a look. He was telling me the truth. The place is a mess. Even the legs have been broken off of the tables." Ware shook his head. "Pure meanness, Boss. That's all it is is pure meanness."

"Bucky didn't see anybody there? He doesn't know who did it?" Longarm asked.

"No, sir. Said he doesn't, and I believe him."

"Did he see anybody suspicious this evening? Did you?"

Again Ware shook his head. "I've wracked my brain about this, Boss, and I just can't think of anybody as would do such a thing. Can't think of why neither."

Threats, gunfire, and now this, Longarm thought. Someone sure as hell wanted him out of the saloon business.

Ira Collins claimed to want to reap profit from the Star. Yet now this had happened.

It did not make sense to him.

Longarm sighed. "We'd best go over there and take a look. Just a quick look. Then we start cleaning up. We want to be open for business . . ." He thought for a moment then said, "No later than noon, Bob. That's our target. We'll have customers coming in by noon. We need to be ready for them."

Ware nodded but did not move. Longarm looked at him and raised an eyebrow. "Well?"

The manager grinned. "Don't you think you should put some clothes on before we go over there, Boss?"

Chapter 46

If anything, Robert Ware had underestimated the damage that had been done by the vandals. In addition to the spilled beer, broken glassware, and ruined tables, a newly installed back-bar mirror was shattered, the floorboards behind the bar were beginning to warp due to the beer spillage, and half a dozen lamps had been broken and whatever oil was in them allowed to run out onto the floor to join the beer there.

It was, simply put, a disaster.

"Brooms and mops will be the first order of the day," Longarm said. "And that carpenter . . . what was his name? The fella that built the bar and the tables? We'll need him to put those tables back together or to build new ones, whichever works out best."

"Jimmy Andrews," Ware said. "That was his name."

"Do you know where to find him?" Longarm asked.

Ware nodded. "Yes, I think so."

"Go get him, please. And where's Bucky anyway? We need him here to help with the cleanup."

"Bucky is probably sleeping by now."

"He can sleep some other time. Right now we need him here," Longarm snapped.

"I'll shake Bucky out on my way to find Andrews," Ware said.

"Go on then," Longarm said. "I'll grab a broom and see if I can't make a dent in this shit. Oh, and on your way back after you get those two moving, stop at Morrison's hardware and buy a new lock. That one seems to be busted all to hell an' gone."

Four hours later the Star was back in business. A fresh keg of beer had been brought up from the cellar, another crate of glassware had been opened, and several trips had been made to various mercantiles to replace broken or missing articles.

"I think we're ready to open the doors again," Longarm announced, "thanks to you fellows. An' I do thank you. I want you to know that. The both o' you pitched in an' made this possible. Robert, you're in charge now. Bucky, you should go home an' get some sleep. You deserve it. Something else you both deserve is a bonus. You'll see that when you get paid this month. I'm putting in extra for the both o' you."

Ware unlocked the newly installed deadbolt and pulled one side of the street door open, then the other, while Longarm grabbed the bung starter and screwed a new spigot into the beer keg.

Jimmy Andrews was still working at building new tables, but the bar was clear and a fresh spread of free lunch laid out.

Within a few minutes the customers started drifting in.

No, dammit, Longarm thought, this saloonkeeping was harder to do than being a deputy United States marshal, no doubt about it.

Chapter 47

"Is there any point to making a formal complaint with Sheriff Anderson?" Longarm mused aloud that evening. He was sitting in Helen's office with a cheroot in one hand and a glass of rye whiskey in the other. It was the first time that day that he had had a chance to sit down and relax.

"Custis!" Helen said. "I'm ashamed of you. Surely you know better than that. Bert Anderson is as useless as tits on a boar hog, and you know it." She shuddered. "Besides which, the man gives me the heebie-jeebies."

"So where do people go around here if they want to get justice?" Longarm asked.

Helen shrugged. "They go to Ira Collins, of course. He runs the town. Most of it anyway. He's as close to being the law as anything we've got. Much as I hate to admit it, Ira is a damn sight better at keeping order than Bert Anderson ever has been."

Longarm grunted unhappily. "Dammit, Helen, Collins is likely the one who ordered my place to be torn up like that to begin with. There's no point in complainin' to him about it when he's the one who caused it."

"You don't *know* who did it, Custis," Helen ponted out. "Surely you of all people would understand the need for proper evidence when it comes to things like this."

He took a deep swallow of the whiskey and scowled. "Yeah, you gotta have proof and all that bullshit. But that's talking 'bout the proper law. That's when some other son of a bitch's ox is being gored. Now it's me an' mine, and that makes it feel a whole lot different."

Longarm sucked on his cheroot for a moment and then tossed back the rest of the rye.

"You look angry, Custis."

"Hell, I am. I am well and truly pissed off, Helen. You should've seen the mess they made. An' they wasted a hell of a lot of beer an' whiskey too. I'd think you would be madder'n me about it all. After all, you're the one who is paying the bills over there." He gestured in the general direction of the Star Saloon.

"If it helps solve my problem," Helen said, "it will be worth every penny and then some." She smiled. "Besides, it should be a good investment in the long run. Right now my whole livelihood depends on these whorehouses. It isn't a bad idea to own a saloon or two. You know. In case some stupid old bastard decides he can regulate people's morality by outlawing whoring. No one has ever been able to stop it, not in all of history, but they keep trying. All they manage to do is to drive it underground. But it still goes on. It always will."

"Of course," Longarm agreed. "You got any more o' this whiskey, darlin'? I could use me a refill." He held his glass out for Helen to freshen.

"What will you do now, Custis?" she asked.

Longarm shrugged. "Damn if I know. But don't you worry none. I'll think of something."

Chapter 48

Bucky Doyle was behind the bar at the Star when Longarm returned to the saloon that night.

"I didn't realize it was so late," Longarm told him. "Robert has gone home for the night?"

Bucky nodded. "He left about an hour ago. Is that all right?"

"Of course," Longarm said. "I know you can handle things. Has anything important happened?"

"Not really. Jimmy finished fixing the tables. He had to replace a couple of the table legs, but most of them could be put back on. I went ahead and paid him out of the cash drawer. I hope that's all right too."

"Just fine," Longarm assured him. "Give me a deck of those cards, would you."

Longarm took the cards and a beer to one of the reconstructed tables and sat down to play a little solitaire and watch over the place.

Not that he actually expected more trouble, but . . .

"Aw, shit!" he blurted as a fight broke out in the back of the place.

Between two of the whores!

The two of them—he could not immediately see which two—were down in the sawdust, rolling, punching, pinching, and, as far as he could tell, biting each other too.

These were not some of Helen's best whores, and Custis Long simply did not know how to ride herd on them in order to prevent the occasional outburst.

He jumped up, leaving his unfinished game of cards and a couple inches of beer.

"Hold on there, you," he barked, standing over the pair of scrapping hookers. He grabbed the shoulder of the one who happened to be on top and yanked the painted bawd away from a younger and much prettier girl.

"This cunt was trying to steal my man," the older whore bawled.

"He likes me better, you old bitch." The younger whore—she called herself Jenny but her real name could have been anything except that—scrambled to her feet and made a lunge for Beauty, who in fact was no beauty and probably never had been.

Longarm shoved Beauty aside and intercepted Jenny's assault. "Calm down, dammit, the both o' you."

He looked around at the ring of curious onlookers who had gathered in the back of the room to watch the women fight. "Who is it that's the cause of all this?" he demanded.

A slim, rough-dressed miner stepped forward. "Me. I think."

"Do you want one o' these girls?" Longarm asked.

"Not now I don't," the miner said, washing his hands of the whole thing.

"Billy!" the older whore bleated. "You and me, Billy. You're my date, honey."

Billy gave the whore a look of pure disgust, turned, and left the place.

"What about me, Billy?" Jenny called after him. "Don't you want me now?"

Apparently he did not, for he left the Star without looking back. Longarm did not blame the man. It would take a complete idiot to get into the middle of that mess a second time.

"Now you see," he told them. "You get to fighting like that an' nobody makes any money. Including me. Now settle down or I'll have to get rid of you."

"You can't do that," Beauty said. "We don't work for you."

"You do as long as you're workin' this place," Longarm snapped.

"Fine. Then I quit. You don't know a damn thing about how to handle us girls," Beauty screamed.

She was probably right, Longarm conceded. He did not know jack shit about whores or how to handle them. Thank goodness for Helen Morrow and her expertise on the subject.

Beauty stormed out of the Star while Jenny just looked frightened. Longarm suspected that Jenny had nowhere else to go and no place else to turn, while a whore Beauty's age likely had plenty of experience to draw on. He had been told that she even had a husband and children somewhere in town.

"All right, everybody," he said, raising his voice. "Fight's over now. Finish up with whatever you're drinking. I'm shutting the place down for the night. We'll be open again tomorrow morning bright an' early."

Chapter 49

Longarm's eyes felt gritty, as if someone had thrown a handful of sand into them. His back ached and his butt was sore. He had spent the night in the saloon, trying to stay alert but dozing off in fits and starts. In the pale light of morning he felt like shit.

He stood, knees cracking loudly, and hobbled over to the bar, where the remains of last night's free lunch stood in fly-specked grandeur. Longarm cut off a chunk of hard, yellow rat cheese. The cheese was dry and begged for something to help wash it down—a trait that made it ideal for a saloon to offer—but all he had behind the bar was beer and whiskey. Neither of those sounded particularly appetizing at that hour. What he wanted was a breakfast, not hard cheese.

Hard cheese would just have to do for the time being.

He heard a key turn in the lock on one of the front doors.

Longarm had his Colt in hand when Bob Ware came inside. He quickly slipped the .45 back into its leather. He doubted that Ware had noticed.

"Boss. What are you doing here at this hour?"

Longarm yawned. "Mornin', Bob. I, uh, I spent the night here. Thought it was just possible the vandals who broke us up the other night might come back an' have another go at us."

"I take it no one showed," Ware said.

"No, but the sons o' bitches might come again. If they do, I want to get a look at them. Maybe throw a little lead in their direction an' get back at them for all the damage they done."

"Will you be spending more nights here then?"

Longarm nodded. "Some."

"Would you like for me to stay with you?"

"No." Longarm smiled. "One of us needs to be awake to tend the bar during the day. I'll be leaning on you to do that for the next little while."

"Whatever you want, Boss. But you look awfully tired," Bob Ware said.

"At the very least I'm gonna bring me a pillow so my ass won't hurt so bad. These damn chairs are hard in case you hadn't noticed."

Ware said, "I can take care of things now, Custis. Why don't you go home and get yourself some sleep? Lord knows you look like you can use it."

"Use it an' then some," Longarm agreed. "All right. I'm gonna go grab some sleep. I'll be back, oh, after lunch. I'll relieve you then an' take over until Bucky gets here for the night shift."

"Take your time. If worse comes to worst, I can always eat the free lunch," Ware said.

"Just stay away from the cheese. It's terrible," Longarm said over his shoulder. He was already on his way to the Pickering and the comfort of a proper bed.

Chapter 50

On Sunday, the fourth night of Longarm's vigil, he heard boots on the boards a half hour or so after Bucky extinguished the lamps and locked up.

Longarm's first thought was relief. He had had a niggling question whether Bob Ware or Bucky Doyle might have in some way been complicit in the destruction. Ira Collins had recommended them, after all, and Longarm barely knew them.

Either of the men could have tipped off the vandals. Both knew that Longarm was keeping watch inside the Star overnight. If someone tried to break in now, it meant that Bob and Bucky were both loyal. So in a way it was a relief to hear the approach of someone now.

He waited. Heard the dull crunch of the lock and mortise being shattered by a pry bar. Saw the intrusion of pale moonlight when the door swung open. Saw two dark shapes fill the doorway and half heard the whispers as the pair felt their way awkwardly into the deeper darkness indoors.

"No, wait. Careful. There's something here. Don't trip over it," a voice whispered.

"You got a match?" the other answered.

"Yeah. Where's a lamp?"

"Over here. I found a lamp but I got no match."

"Just a second. I . . . There."

Longarm heard the scrape and saw the sudden flare of light as the match was struck and quickly applied to the wick of a wall lamp.

"Shit, I burnt my fucking finger," one of them mumbled before he adjusted the lamp wick to a bright yellow butterfly.

"Where do you want to start, eh?"

"First thing, I want to set aside some of these bottles of whiskey. We can take a few with us when we leave."

"Good idea. Those would be over . . . Oh, shit!"

Longarm peered at them over the barrel of his .45. "Evenin', boys."

In the light they had so helpfully provided he could see that these were the same two he had seen in Ira Collins's outer office. They were, or so he presumed, George Stepanek's cronies.

"Stand easy now, an' I'll find you each a nice jail cell to sleep in," Longarm said.

Not that he had any idea where he might find that jail cell. Or any lawman tending it. There was neither jail nor lawman in town here, although he supposed he could put the two in handcuffs, load them onto the next train through, and cart them off to some larger burg for trial.

He would worry about that later. His first priority now had to be the handcuffs. Everything else would come after.

"Hands high an' turn yourselves around, boys," he said.

The fellow who had lighted the lamp, a tall, beefy man with a red complexion and heavy stubble that was just short of being a beard, dutifully lifted his hands shoulder high.

The other, however, hesitated. He was thin and wiry with dark blond hair and a carefully trimmed pencil mustache.

"Don't . . . ," Longarm warned.

Too late. The fellow snatched his pistol out of its leather.

He must have thought himself quick with a gun. And in fact he was very fast.

On the other hand, no one is faster on the draw than a .45 that is already in hand and aimed at him. It was a lesson learned the hard way.

Before the intruder's revolver cleared the leather, Longarm's Colt belched flame and smoke.

And lead.

The slug hit the son of a bitch high in the belly, just under the breastbone, just under the heart.

The man grunted, the sound driven out of him with the impact. He looked down at himself, his expression puzzled with disbelief.

By that time his companion stood transfixed, hand poised over the grips of his gun but panic showing plain on his face. He hesitated, then spun around, and bolted for the open doorway.

Longarm could have dropped the son of a bitch. His finger tightened on the trigger, but at the last instant he chose to hold his fire. He knew who the man was and could find him when he wanted him.

In the meantime . . .

He put another bullet into the first man, who still had his gun in hand.

Longarm's slug raised a puff of dust from the fellow's coat, the bullet striking low on his right side. The impact turned him half around. His knees sagged and then let go altogether, dropping him to the floor. He toppled facedown into the sawdust, his not-quite-fast-enough Colt unfired.

Longarm crossed the saloon floor in a hurry and kicked the man's gun away—he was dying but not yet dead and might still have found the strength to pull a trigger—before kneeling beside him.

"Your partner ran out on you," Longarm said. "Where's he gone?"

The dying man was ghostly pale, his skin yellowed and filmed with oily sweat.

"Where?" Longarm repeated.

If the man heard, he gave no indication of it. His whole attention was directed inward. Likely thinking of his own belly and the fact that he could no longer draw breath.

There was practically no blood coming from his wounds. There must have been plenty flooding his gut, but it was not leaking outside of his body.

At the last moment he looked up at Longarm. Then the life went out of his eyes and he exhaled for the last time on this side of the great divide.

"Shit," Longarm mumbled. He wanted to talk to the intruders, not kill them.

He was not going to talk to this one, that was certain. There was, however, the other.

Longarm stood and stepped out into the cool evening air. A three-foot-long pry bar was leaned against the wall where the two had left it. He shoved his Colt back into his holster and looked up and down the street, wondering which way the other vandal had fled.

The only sound in the night was the very distant wail and rattle of a train rolling through the darkness.

The depot, Longarm thought. If that man really wanted to get away, there were only two directions he might logically go. One would be toward Ira Collins, seeking sanctuary from his boss. The other would be toward getting the hell out of town. And a train would present the best opportunity for that.

If he ran to Collins, Longarm would be able to find him at his leisure.

And if to the train . . .

Longarm pulled the broken door shut behind him and started a slow and cautious walk toward the railroad depot, alert just in case the rabbit had not gone to ground but wanted to show some fight instead.

Chapter 51

There! A dark shape detached itself from the shadows at the loading chutes and scuttled hurriedly to a boxcar just as the train began to move, pulling away from the depot.

Longarm had been sitting on the platform keeping watch for more than an hour. Now the wait was paying off.

He stood and hitched up his britches, then stepped forward to stand beside the tracks.

He waited as the cars began to clatter past, keeping his eye on the car where the shadow had disappeared. There were four boxcars in this train. The one he wanted was the second.

As it reached him, Longarm grabbed the open doorway and swung up into the dark car. The man he wanted to talk to was somewhere in—

The back end of the car was lighted up as the muzzle flash of a pistol shot flared bright, and a large-caliber bullet slammed into the wood of the siding not two feet from Longarm's head.

Longarm's response was immediate. His .45 came into hand and he returned fire.

A man screamed in pain. And shot at Longarm a second time.

Longarm's Colt was already in hand this time, and his return fire was almost instantaneous. He threw his shot close beside the muzzle flash from the back of the car.

The rumble of iron wheels was loud and the car shook and clattered as it passed over the rails.

Longarm threw himself forward, seeking the shadows away from the open doorway. He waited but the noises around him were too loud for him to expect to hear anything short of another pistol shot, and he could not see the figure at the back of the car.

There was no exit other than the open door, and Longarm could clearly see anything or anyone approaching that. By the same token if he moved to the back of the car, he would likely be silhouetted against the doorway.

He knelt, revolver in hand. And waited.

Chapter 52

Longarm ambled back to the depot. The next train back to Helen's town was due in ten or twelve minutes. He had had plenty of time while he waited to have breakfast, clean his .45, and stroll around this town.

He would have liked to get some sleep, but that would have to wait, lest he miss his train connection. And he damn sure did not want to walk back. He had come a good eighty or a hundred miles during the night, sharing the otherwise empty boxcar with a dead man.

Not that he had been sure about Ira Collins's man, whatever the hell his name had been. He had not relaxed his vigilance until daybreak. That was when he discovered that his shooting during the night had been more lucky than accurate.

His bullet had taken the fellow high on his left leg. It tore through an artery, and the man bled to death, probably within ten minutes or less. There was a hell of a lot of coagulated blood pooled on the floor of the boxcar.

Longarm had gotten off the train the next time it stopped.

He left the dead man where he was. Someone would find him eventually.

As for Ira Collins and George Stepanek . . . he had a bone to pick with those two.

And he intended to take the matter up with them as soon as he got back.

Well, almost as soon. Longarm felt out on his feet. Once he finally got back, he sleepwalked his way to the Pickering and dropped like a rock onto his bed. He did not even wash the soot off himself—the hotel could worry about their own sheets—until seven hours later, when he woke up feeling infinitely better.

It was dark when he woke, so he sat up and felt around on the bedside table for the block of matches, prized one off, and struck it alight. He lifted the globe of the lamp and touched the flame to its wick, spreading a soft yellow light through the whole room.

He poured water into the basin and washed himself before he dressed. He needed a shave, but that would have to wait. He was not sure of the time, but it was pitch-dark outside his window and the barbershop was sure to be closed for the night.

Helen Morrow's whorehouses, on the other hand, would be open for business at this hour.

Longarm checked his .45, grabbed his Stetson, and headed for Helen's best house.

It probably no longer mattered if he was seen as her ally, but it did no harm if he were mistaken for a customer.

He briefly detoured past the Star, but the lights there were bright, and he could see Bucky behind the bar. Fortunately Bob Ware and Bucky were entirely capable of running the place without the boss interfering; both of them knew a hell of a lot more about the saloon business than Longarm ever would.

"I'd like to see Miss Morrow," he told the stunning little redhead—small girl, big tits—who greeted him at the door. "I know the way."

"Yes, sir." The girl curtsied and gave him a dimpled smile, then disappeared back into the parlor in search of someone interested in paying for her services.

Longarm watched her ass twitch from side to side until the girl was out of sight.

Then he headed back toward Helen's now familiar office.

Chapter 53

"Any more letters?" Longarm asked once he had a glass of rye under his belt and a cheroot smoldering in the ashtray beside him.

"Six," Helen said as she poured a refill for him. "All the same bullshit. All in the same hand. I burned them."

"But no one has tried to break up one of your houses or beat up your girls? Nothing like that?"

She shook her head, her jowls fluttering when she did so. She went back to her chair, reinforced to take her weight without breaking. "I heard about your place being broken up, of course. Heard you got back at the ones who did it, too. What happened that you disappeared like you did. Bobby was convinced they had murdered you and hid the body somewhere."

"Bobby?" Longarm said, grinning.

"You know that I know everyone, Custis. I call him Bobby because my girls do."

"I thought Bob was married," Longarm said.

"He is. What's your point?" Helen shot back at him.

"Nothing. Sorry."

"So what are you going to do, Custis? Short of staying on as a saloon owner, that is. And what did they do to make you disappear like that?"

He took a swallow of his rye and a puff on the cheroot before he answered. Then he told her about his night. And his unplanned trip in a boxcar.

"He's dead, you say?" Helen said.

Longarm nodded. "Cold as a trout."

"That leaves only George and Ira. What do you plan to do about them?"

"First thing I'm gonna do . . . first thing tomorrow morning, that is . . . will be to go have me a little talk with Collins. I figure to give him a bill for damages. The son of a bitch cost me . . . forgive me, cost *you* . . . a pretty penny to get all that breakage cleaned up an' replaced." Longarm shrugged. "He's the one who broke it; he's the one who can replace it. Seems only fair."

Helen laughed. "You have a pair on you, Custis. Ira has a choke hold on this town, and he is greedy for more. I don't think anyone has ever really stood up to him."

"Then it's about time someone did," Longarm said, finishing his whiskey. His grin flashed again, and he stood up, setting his empty glass down. "I can't go see the man till morning, so I was wondering, could I borrow that little redhead for a few hours? Or, um, the rest o' the night?"

A flash of something—pain?—flickered across Helen's face, and it occurred to Longarm, too late, that while they were no longer lovers she might still think of him that way. It might have hurt her to realize that he wanted one of her whores to drain his balls now instead of her.

It was too late to take the request back, although he would

not have caused Helen pain for love nor money, certainly not deliberately.

"Her working name is Betty, but her real name is Elsie. Come with me, Custis. We'll get her. No charge, of course." Helen smiled. "I'm sure you will like her."

Helen took Longarm by the hand and led him toward the parlor.

Chapter 54

Longarm went to breakfast the next morning smelling of perfume and face powder and feeling about as thoroughly relaxed as he had in quite some time.

He found a fly-specked little café a block from Helen's whorehouse and surrounded a well-done steak and a mountain of fried potatoes, poured half a gallon of black coffee down his gullet, and pronounced himself fit for any damn thing that came along.

Including Ira Collins.

Longarm marched into Collins's office ready to whip wildcats with his bare hands. He was ready for . . . He was *not* ready for what he found.

The person at Collins's reception desk was a kid, a boy probably fourteen or fifteen years old, with a shock of blond hair and a very serious manner.

"Your business, sir?"

"I want to see Mr. Collins," Longarm told the boy.

"And this would be about . . . ?"

"I suppose you'd say that I have a complaint to make," Longarm said.

"We have a form for that," the boy said, frowning. "At least . . . I think we do. Let me look." He got up from behind the desk and began rummaging through a file cabinet.

"No form," Longarm said. "I need to see that man face-to-face. Him an' that son of a bitch Stepanek too."

The boy looked to be startled, perhaps by Longarm's choice of language.

Good Lord, Longarm wondered, was I ever that young? Probably not, but then Longarm had grown up at a time of warfare and wholesale bloodshed.

"Wait here a second, sir." The boy stepped a few paces to the closed door into Collins's office, opened it far enough to stick his head inside, and loudly bellowed, "Dad! There's a man out here to see you. He insists."

Dad. It explained quite a lot.

It also presented something of a problem. Longarm did not want to be put in the position of having to gun a man down in front of his son. And he would not, not unless he absolutely was forced to.

He could not hear what Collins had to say to the boy, but the kid returned, leaving the door open.

"He'll see you now, sir."

"Thank you, son." Longarm winked at the boy and went in to find Ira Collins sitting behind a small stack of ledger books.

"Mr. Long. What can I do for you today?"

Longarm glanced back over his shoulder. The door was still open. The boy, Ira Collins's son, was standing there, obviously wanting to participate in the family business as much as he could.

That fact changed Longarm's plans. He had intended to come on hard with the man. Now . . .

"We need to talk," he said.

Chapter 55

"I was sorry to hear that someone broke into your place and broke up everything they could," Collins said before Longarm could start in on him. "I don't know who could do such a thing."

Longarm scowled. He was acutely aware of the boy standing there, but . . . "Your people done that," he said, careful to keep his voice calm.

"Mine?" Collins seemed genuinely puzzled. "Why in the world would I have my people do such a thing?"

"I reckon for the same reason you're tryin' to drive Helen Morrow out o' business here," Longarm said.

"Drive Miss Morrow out of business? Mr. Long, now you have me thoroughly confused. Why, I have no more desire to do that than to cause you harm. I don't know Miss Morrow well, but she seems very pleasant and very capable. She runs honest houses. Her, um," he glanced toward his son, "her employees cause no trouble, and their presence generates business for establishments that I have an interest in. If anything, she is an asset to the community.

Not in the normally accepted sense, perhaps, but she is an asset nonetheless. Besides, she has every right to conduct whatever business she pleases, and I support her right to do so."

"Now I'm the one that's confused," Longarm said. "I mean, you sound sincere in what you're sayin' there, but it don't fit with the things I've heard about you an' your business practices."

Collins smiled. "I drive as hard a bargain as I can get away with, Long. You've experienced it yourself. But when you and I sat down to talk about your rental on that building you are in, I didn't dictate to you. You and I negotiated. We arrived at an agreeable solution to the matter at hand, and both of us have stuck by it. Isn't that true?"

Longarm nodded. "Aye, I reckon it is."

"I'm that way in all my dealings," Collins said.

"I could almost believe you," Longarm said, "except for Stepanek an' his bullyboys."

"Bullyboys? I don't understand."

"Him an' all the trouble they've caused is what I mean," Longarm said. "The bullying an' the beatings an' the robberies."

"I know of no robberies," Collins said. "Not committed by any of my people anyway."

"Huh." Longarm pushed his hat back and rubbed his head. "They jumped me when I first got here. Stole every penny I had on me. An' it was your people that did it. Stepanek put them up to it, I'm thinking."

"I am truly sorry, Mr. Long, but if George or his people did anything like that, believe me, I will get rid of them this instant." He turned to his son and said, "Donny, go find Mr. Stepanek. Have him and those friends of his come here right away. No matter what they are doing, they are to stop it and come right here."

"Yes, sir." The boy spun around and raced out of the building.

When they were alone, Collins said, "Are you sure about your accusation, Mr. Long?"

"I'm sure. And it ain't *Mister* Long. It's Deputy United States Marshal Long." Longarm pulled out his wallet and flipped it open to display his credentials. "I'm here trying to work out if you're breaking any laws in your dealings here, Mr. Collins."

"Mist . . . excuse me, Deputy Long, you or any of your people are welcome to look at my books now or at any other time. I try to run an honest business. I know nothing, I promise you nothing, about any strong-arm tactics. If my people damaged you in any way, I will be glad to reimburse you for your loss."

Longarm grunted. "What about all the letters?" he asked.

"Letters? Again, Deputy, you have me confused. I don't know anything about any letters."

Longarm briefly told him about the notes Helen and her working girls had been getting. "I got two myself," Longarm said.

"Believe me, sir, if George or his people did anything like that . . ."

Now Collins was referring to the sidekicks as Stepanek's people, Longarm noticed.

"You don't have to worry about them," he said. "The both of them managed to get themselves dead."

Collins looked pale. "Dead! I . . . I don't condone violence, Deputy. Never. Nothing like that was ever done at my direction. Never."

His tone of voice, his expression . . . Longarm believed him. He was surprised, but in fact he believed Ira Collins.

But why would George Stepanek and "his" people strong-arm the community on their own.

Perhaps they would get their answers when Donny Collins got back with Stepanek.

Chapter 56

Donny Collins came running back, the left side of his face red and swelling, unspent tears glistening in the corners of his eyes, although he was trying to hold them back so as to not seem unmanly.

Collins jumped out from behind his desk and hurried to meet and comfort his son. "What the devil has happened, Donny? Who did this?"

"Mr. George, did it, Dad. I told him you wanted to see him right away, and he asked me why. He asked me who you were talking to and what they were saying. I didn't think there would be anything wrong with telling him. So I did. And he got m-mad and he h-hit me. Hard."

The unshed tears flowed then. The kid was not able to contain them any longer, and soon he was sobbing.

Collins put his arms around his son and held on to him.

"Where is Mr. George?" Longarm said. "If you don't mind me askin', that is."

Donny first looked up at his father, who nodded for him to answer. "He was heading for the livery stable," the boy said.

Longarm raised an eyebrow. "Where's that, Ira?"

"The edge of town. Two blocks in that dir—"

Before he could finish the directions, Longarm had passed through the office doorway and was halfway across the anteroom.

George Stepanek was busy saddling a sleek roan when Longarm strode into the livery barn. "Goin' somewhere, George?"

Stepanek swung around to face him, blood in the man's eye, his face red with barely contained fury. "You son of a bitch. You've ruined everything. Until you came and messed things up, I was on my way to owning those whorehouses and most of Ira's properties too. Then you, you bastard, you had to stick your ugly nose in."

"First off, George, Helen Morrow is a friend of mine. Anything that hurts her is gonna piss me off *real* bad. Second, poking my nose in where somebody else don't want it is what I do for a living. I'm a deputy United States marshal, and I'm wondering if you've broken any laws that I can arrest you for.

"Come to think of it, George, I expect the sensible thing for me to do is to put you in cuffs and haul you off to jail while I finish figuring that out." Longarm smiled. "So what say you turn around and put your hands behind you."

"No damned way, Long. Is that your real name anyway? It's really Long?"

"It's really Long, George, and you are under arrest."

"What the hell for?"

"Jeez, George, I don't care. How about inciting to riot? Would that work for you?"

"But I haven't done . . ."

"Oh, I think maybe you have. So I'm gonna take you in, George. We'll work out the exact charges after I go over the county records to see what all you've stolen and from who," Longarm said, relaxed and smiling.

Stepanek made the mistake of thinking the casual expression meant Longarm's guard was down.

The man grabbed for his gun.

The simpleton had already had one demonstration that he was not Custis Long's equal with a .45.

He made that mistake again.

It was his last.

Longarm's Colt belched fire and smoke and lead. The bullet punched a hole the size of a dime—a red and bloody dime—almost squarely between George Stepanek's eyes.

The man's head snapped back, and a red mist of blood and bone and brains fanned out behind his head.

Stepanek tottered backward half a step. Then he collapsed. The man's knees buckled, and he toppled face-forward into a pile of fresh horse shit.

Longarm looked down at what was left of Stepanek. "Couldn't happen to a nicer son of a bitch, Georgie," he mumbled as he punched the empty out of his Colt and dropped a fresh cartridge into the cylinder.

Ira Collins caught up with him near the depot. "Where are you going, Long?"

"First off I need to get a wire off to my boss in Denver. Gotta tell him that I'll be back on the job in a day or two. Then I need to get you and Helen together. She thinks it's you who've been after her properties. You need to let her know that isn't so."

Longarm chuckled. "After that, Ira, I'm gonna take me a day . . . more like a night . . . just to myself. Well, to me an' a certain little redhead that I know. Now, if you will excuse me, I got that wire to send."

Longarm touched the brim of his Stetson, then turned and resumed his march toward the telegraph office.